ASK ME AGAIN

GINA L. MAXWELL

Jenny ~
I hope you enjoy
my sister's love story!
Gina L. Maxwell

Content and Line Editing: Kristin Anders, www.TheRomanticEditor.com

Formatting and Cover Design: Kerrie Legend at www.kerrielegend.com.

❀ Created with Vellum

To my baby sister, Tricia, whose own love story was the basis for this book.
Thank you for your unconditional support, friendship, and love.
(And for giving me artistic license to radically change some things for the good of the story.)
I wish you and TJ a lifetime of love and happiness, Shorty.
Love you more than double fudge chocolate ice cream with dark chocolate shavings...
~ Me ~
Also to my amazing friend, KP, without whom this book would not make a lick of sense.

CHAPTER ONE

Three thousand four hundred and twenty-six.

That's how many days of her life Trish Howell wasted with a man who broke up with her because *he* decided it was "for her own good." She still couldn't believe that after more than nine years of planning their lives together—marriage, children, big house away from the city where they'd host barbeques for their city-dwelling friends—Nick had ended it all in a single conversation.

It wasn't as if their demise had been obvious with little disagreements escalating into bigger arguments. If they'd been fighting maybe it wouldn't have felt like, after a decade of building a life together, he suddenly hit her over the head with a damn two-by-four.

As it happened, he'd kissed her in the morning before she headed off to her small yet thriving aesthetician business. After a long day at work, they'd enjoyed a nice dinner together then settled in to watch their favorite shows. But Nick must not have been in the mood for *How I Met Your Mother* that night, because instead of turning on the TV, he turned *off* their relationship.

No brief satellite interruptions, no blue screen while the

system rebooted for another try, no customer service number to call for technical support.

Just...off.

Now Trish's once-successful life consisted of shacking up with her older sister Rhianna, her husband, and their two teenage kids in the dinky town she grew up in, while working as a waitress/bartender at Paddy's, the local Irish pub. *Insult, meet Injury.*

Trish pulled the lever for the Guinness on tap and watched the dark liquid fill the glass in a daze. That's how she'd moved through the world for the last two weeks since leaving her life behind in New York City. She only had two settings: dazed in public, and broken in private.

Picking up her tray of drinks, she walked around the end of the bar and wound her way through the tables filled with Friday night customers to get to the six-top in the back corner. She dropped off their drinks and checked on her other tables before stopping at a four-top that had just swapped inhabitants.

"Evening, everyone," she said, pulling out her notepad. "Can I start by getting you some drinks while you look over the menu?"

"Oh my goodness, is that little Trish Howell?"

Trish looked up in the direction of the feminine voice and barely stopped herself from wincing. "Hi, Mrs. Madsen, how are you?" Mrs. Madsen was a friend of the family. The kind who had chats with Trish's mom after church, and once a year their families got together for a barbeque and pool party.

"Your mom told me about what happened with you and Nick, you poor thing, but I didn't know you were moving back home." Then to the three other ladies at the table Mrs. Madsen clarified, "She would have told me, but we haven't had time to talk at church the last couple of weeks." Mrs. Madsen turned her curious gaze back to Trish. "I bet you're glad to be back, aren't you, dear?"

Trish did her best to lift the corners of her mouth into some semblance of a smile. "Words can't express how it feels to be back, Mrs. Madsen." Her crushed dreams and wounded pride said it all.

"You're so sweet. Well, wait till I tell Henry you're home and working here at Paddy's..."

Trish tuned out the rest of Mrs. Madsen's plans for filling her husband in on the town grapevine's news of the prodigal daughter's return. She focused on holding her tight smile and nodded every so often to continue the pretense of listening, then made an excuse about waiting customers and promised to be back shortly to take their order.

She took cover behind the bar where she'd be able to keep herself busy washing glasses and restocking supplies with limited customer interaction for a while. Noticing the garnishes needed refreshing, she grabbed several limes and began slicing them into even sections. Erin, the young owner of the pub and an old high school friend, emerged from the back room and joined Trish.

"Hey, hon, how you holding up?" Erin shot her a brief concerned look as she grabbed two used glasses, dipped them into the deep sink of hot, soapy water then into the sanitized water before setting them on the drying rack.

Shrugging a shoulder, Trish said, "I'm fine. Still readjusting to small town life."

She kept her focus on dividing the limes perfectly. Unlike how her life had been divided up by her break up with Nick. It'd been like a divorce where he had a high-powered attorney and she a public defender in a cheap suit. Nick got their apartment in Astoria, all of their new furniture—which *she'd* bought because her credit was better—and all of their friends.

Then, as if losing all that hadn't been a big enough kick in the junk, she'd lost her aesthetician business. She'd been so proud of herself, taking the leap to start her own company. She worked hard to grow her clientele and earned a reputation as one of the leading aestheticians in Queens. Clients traveled from other

Burroughs and even New Jersey because they preferred her to anyone else.

But with no apartment, no relationship, and no more friends, Trish moved back to her hometown Podunk, Wisconsin, and that meant she had to sell her business. She deposited the entire amount into a new savings account where it would stay until she needed startup stash for her new venture. She loved being a business owner, and wanted to do it again someday.

Hence, her need for the tiny wages and fluctuating tips of this job to cover the only bill she currently had, her cell phone, and she insisted on paying something to Rhianna for letting her stay with them.

All she needed now was a clue as to where she should make all that happen.

WHAT A SHITTY DAY. If there was ever a night Tony DiAngelo needed to have a beer or ten, it was this one. Not only had the day job exhausted him—trying to get middle schoolers to pay attention three weeks before summer break was a teacher's Mission: Impossible—but on his way to coach his soccer team, old Mrs. Danvers t-boned him and messed up the passenger side of his car. After dealing with the headache of talking to the police and his insurance company, he finally arrived at the game only to find his co-ed kindergarteners acting like there was a full moon, officially making his day one big clusterfuck.

Tony nodded to Jason, his good friend and the ref for the youth soccer games, who was waiting outside for him at their favorite bar in town. The original owners of Paddy's Pub were old townies who sold it to one of Tony's friends from school. It was one of those places that everyone frequented on a regular basis. The small size made it cramped as hell sometimes, but no one ever seemed to mind. There were plenty of other great local hangouts in the small town of Fort Atkinson, but none of them matched the atmosphere and good company of Paddy's.

Pulling open the heavy wooden door, Tony stepped inside and drew in a deep breath of the heavenly aroma of beer and fried cheese curds. He could almost feel the tension of the day start to slip from his shoulders.

Jason tapped him on the arm to get his attention. "Hey, order me a beer. I'll grab us a table."

Finding a rare open seat at the far end of the sturdy counter that ran the length of the room, Tony looked for the closest bartender to help make the end of his night bearable. A brunette with a killer body was working all the way at the other end. Tony's starved libido woke up and yanked on its short tether. It'd been a long time since he'd been tempted to unleash it, but from what he could see, this girl could tempt him straight to hell and he wouldn't give a damn.

Her black leggings left only the color of her skin beneath them to the imagination. They flaunted every delicious curve from hip to calf where her tall black boots took over. Instead of the dark green Paddy's T-shirt the employees were typically outfitted in, she wore a pink shirt so thin that her black tank underneath showed through and hung off her right shoulder. Lazy dark brown curls swung over her back. Flashes of them raked up by his fingers or maybe wrapped around his hand flooded his mind.

Christ, if he kept this up, the bar wouldn't be the only hard wood in front of him. How long had it been since he'd had sex? A year? *Too long, obviously.* Now he understood why people who were lost in the desert saw visions with pools of cool water. Imaginations were cruel bastards.

So who the hell *was* she? Erin must have hired her recently, yet she didn't act like a new hire, on edge and unsure of herself. She moved easily in the space and mixed drinks instinctively, her hands doing all the work as she talked with the customers.

"Did you win the big game tonight, Coach?"

Pulled from his thoughts, Tony turned to his friend and owner of Paddy's as she placed a Point Beer in front of him. "Hey, Erin. Thanks," he said before taking several long pulls on the longneck. The taste of his favorite beer washed some of the day's irritations away, and after draining half the bottle, he released a grateful sigh.

"That bad, huh?" she asked. Erin attended a lot of the games because her niece was on his team, so she knew how things could go from calm to crazy to tears all in a matter of minutes.

He shrugged. "First half was good, but somewhere in the third quarter, I lost them. A boy from the other team bumped into Jessica so she shoved him into a mud puddle. Then Sophia whispered something to Scottie in the huddle. She giggled, he blushed, and the next thing I know, he's picking dandelion bouquets instead of protecting the goal."

Pausing in her wipe down of the perfectly clean counter, she clutched the damp towel to her chest and went full-on girly. "Oh my God, that's so *cute*. He's a doll, that Scottie."

Tony rolled his eyes. "*Not* cute. With Scottie playing Romeo the whole second half, the Mighty Minnows beat the Shark Bytes 4-1, which is doubly embarrassing because of the names." He pointed an accusing finger at Erin. "Romance has no place on the battlefield, woman. If I didn't know better, I'd say Sophia took a bribe to throw the game."

"And what sort of bribe does a five-year-old little girl in pigtails take, exactly?"

"Pudding cups," he deadpanned. Erin laughed and tossed the rag at him, which he caught before it hit his face. "I'm serious. Have you seen the crazed look she gets in her eyes when the parents bring pudding cups for after a game? It's not pretty. I think she has a pudding problem."

Sliding off the stool, Tony winked and downed the rest of his beer. Joking around with Erin and getting his first alcoholic beverage under his belt had lifted his mood considerably.

"Pretend all you want, Tony DiAngelo, but everyone knows you're crazy about those kids."

He sighed dramatically. "Yeah. Those pint-sized gremlins own my ass, and they know it. They've completely destroyed my tough-guy rep with the ladies."

He'd been trying to make a joke, but it fell flat, deflating into a lump at his feet. Erin placed a hand over his and squeezed. "There are worse traits than having a weak spot for kindergarteners, Tony. Personally, I think it's sexy and heart-melting, and the *right* woman will think so, too."

What was that saying girls had? *The good ones are taken and the rest are all gay?* Tony wondered if it worked the same way for women. Sometimes it felt like it, especially when one of the good ones—Erin—said things like that. By her reasoning, his ex-fiancée hadn't been one of the good ones. It had bothered Jennifer that he put so much time and energy into coaching the youth soccer and tee ball teams. She never quite "got" his passion for inspiring and teaching kids a love of sports, and values like teamwork and good sportsmanship, just like his coaches had done for him his whole life.

When she left him, he'd been devastated, but it didn't take him long to realize she'd done them both a favor. They weren't good together. He hadn't even loved her as much as he should for a woman he planned to spend his life with.

Leaning over the bar, Tony kissed Erin's cheek. She was a great friend, and he was glad he decided to go out with Jason tonight instead of heading home to channel surf and settle for leftovers. Tony pulled a few bills from his wallet and handed them to Erin. "I'll take two Points and then we'll need another round whenever you get a chance to toss in an order of your famous cheese curds."

"You got it. I'll put the order in now and bring it back in a few."

"No rush." He started to leave, but then turned around at the last second. He had a better idea. "Actually," he said with a smile, "can you send the new girl back? I'd like to introduce myself and give her a proper welcome to Paddy's. You know how I hate being rude."

Erin's eyebrows shot up. "The new girl?" Her eyes bounced between him and the girl in question still working the other end of the dimly lit bar. "You mean *that* new girl?"

Tony countered with an arched brow of his own and crossed his arms over his chest. He wondered at her hesitation. She'd made "introductions" for him plenty of times, whether he asked her to or not. Erin was a notorious matchmaker, especially with her friends. "I don't know how many you've hired recently, but yes, *that* one with the amazing ass, is who I'm referring to. Is she dating someone already?"

"No," she said carefully. Erin popped the top on a longneck and slid it to a customer a few feet away. Then she did the same thing on two more and set them in front of Tony. "She's actually coming out of a bad breakup, but that's Tr—"

"Perfect," he said, thumping the bar with his hands for emphasis. "She needs a third-party friend to take her out and get her mind off things."

"All right, I'll send her over," she said with a devious grin. "Good luck, hot shot."

"No such thing as luck, Erin. You either got it, or you don't." Tony snagged the open beers and started to back away from the counter with a big grin, pointing to his chest. "And I've got *lots* of it."

Erin laughed and tossed her final retort over her shoulder as she turned to the register. "Good thing, 'cause you're gonna need it."

Tony and Jason sat at a small table against the back wall,

swapping stories about their students—Jason taught Phys Ed at the middle school—and trying to one-up each other, as usual. About ten minutes later, Tony felt a presence behind his right shoulder. Assuming it was another customer milling around, he didn't pay any attention until a hand with French manicured nails reached around him to place two bottles of Point on the table.

New girl. He smirked to himself, wondering how he could've forgotten about the brown-haired beauty tasked with bringing him their next round. Anxious to finally see her up close, he turned to look over his shoulder, but all he saw was her left hand spread beneath the round tray she held. He scowled when he realized she couldn't get to the side of their table because of two guys animatedly sharing a story with their friends at the next table over.

Tony studied his friend's face to gauge his interest since he had a clear view of the woman. Oh, he had plenty of interest. Too much. The guy was working his lady-killer smile, and for the first time, Tony had the urge to punch the man in his pretty face. Tony had dibs, damn it. He'd seen her first.

Shit, maybe he shouldn't try to impress a woman immediately after being with his kids. Their laws and brand of justice seemed to rub off on him.

Once she placed the basket of cheese curds and two small plates in the middle of their table, she started to lower the now-empty tray and asked, "Anything else I can get you guys?"

She'd barely finished her question when one of the drunks next to her side-stumbled, pushing her right onto Tony. He'd seen it in time and twisted his body, catching her to prevent her from falling completely over. She smelled amazing, something floral and exotic and oddly familiar, but he didn't have time to analyze it or enjoy how her soft hips felt in his hands before she pushed off of him with an unnecessary apology.

The guy who'd caused the incident, however, was bitching

about the beer he'd sloshed onto himself and demanded she get him a free replacement. Tony's temper flared like a match struck to life. If there was anything he couldn't abide, it was misogynistic assholes without a chivalrous bone in their bodies.

He scraped back his chair, unfolded to his full six-foot-three-inches, and stepped well into the jerk's personal space. Like all good friends, Jason did the same from the other side, arms crossed and ready to back him up if need be. Wanting to keep the situation contained for Erin's sake, Tony kept his voice low, but made sure it conveyed every bit of his irritation.

"Apologize to her."

"For what?" the man demanded with indignance.

"For not watching where you were going, for being an asshole, or because if you don't, I'm going to take you out back and make you wish you had." He shrugged. "Your pick."

Anger at being dressed down in front of his friends sparked in the man's eyes, but Tony had at least five inches and fifty pounds on the guy, so he wasn't about to act on it. At least he wasn't a *stupid* asshole.

"It's fine," she said at his side. "Accidents happen. Let's not make a big deal out of it, okay?"

The sound of her voice revved Tony's engine something fierce, but he pushed it aside until he handled this. "No, it's not okay," he said. "When a man fucks up, he apologizes. Now, are you a man, or aren't you?"

Glancing over, the ass finally caved with a stiff nod in her direction. "It was my fault. I'm sorry." His eyes swung back to Tony for approval. Tony gave him a chin lift and a look that suggested he make himself scarce. The man turned and trailed after his friend through the bar and out the door. Tony hadn't meant for him to leave, but fine by him.

"I appreciate your sense of honor—even if it *is* a tad extreme —but you didn't have to do that," she said. "I'm not the distressed damsel type, and drunk assholes come with the job. They don't bother me."

That voice. Why did it make him so— Finally, Tony turned to get his first real look at the new girl and froze. His brain short-circuited, his limbs atrophied, and the thoughts whipping around in his head refused to make their way out of his damn face hole.

Trish Howell.

"Holy shit, *Tony?*" Her eyes opened wide in mutual shock, but apparently *he* was the only one who'd gone catatonic. Awesome. She'd be impressed by that for sure.

Trish fucking Howell. She was more beautiful than he remembered. Olive skin, perfectly arched eyebrows, almond-shaped eyes the color of dark chocolate, and full pink lips that stretched into a brilliant smile that made him feel like the only man in a room.

He'd had it bad for her since the third grade when he'd taken her softball glove away from her and she kicked him in the shin for the offense. By the end of recess, they'd become friends, but that shin-kick had started a decade-long crush on one of his closest school friends.

Not that she knew that, of course. Not for sure, anyway. Plenty of people teased them over the years—especially Trish's oldest sister, Rhianna, who enjoyed threatening to break his fingers if he ever made a move on her. But the threats had been moot. Trish had kept him firmly in the friend zone, and he'd been too much of a wuss to tell her how he felt, so in the friend zone he'd stayed.

At last, Tony mentally slapped himself out of his shock. Go, him. Giving her a warm smile, he said, "Little Trish Howell, how the hell are ya? What's it been, what, five years since you've been back home?"

"I'm just peachy, thanks. And you can't call me little if I'm four months older than you."

He didn't miss the fact she'd avoided his second question, but he left it alone. "Not referring to your age, short-stack."

Trish narrowed her eyes. "I seem to remember we were still the same height at graduation, then I came back for Christmas a couple years later and you're suddenly freakishly tall."

He chuckled. "Told you, my family has a history of being late bloomers."

She snorted, and it was kind of adorable. "Late bloomers, my ass. It's no wonder I didn't recognize you. Obviously you paid another visit to whatever mad scientist keeps altering your appearance."

Tony feigned ignorance. "I have no idea what you're talking about."

"Oh, please," she said with a roll of her eyes. "You're *huge*."

Jason interjected with, "Ah, the two little words every man wants to hear. Though she's clearly exaggerating in your case, T."

Without taking his eyes from the now-laughing woman in front of him, Tony raised his arm and flipped his friend off.

"Not like *that*. I mean, no offense, Tony; I don't know if you are or not." Both men opened their mouths—though probably not to say the same thing—but she quickly held her hands up to stop them. "Nor do I *need* to know, boys. I was talking about your *body*. Your *body* got huge. Okay, now it just sounds weird every time I say the word 'huge.' You know what I mean, though, right? Last time I saw you, you weren't so..."

Jason, ever so helpful, decided to chime in between curds. "Muscular? Ripped? Godlike? Sexy? Dreamy?"

"Dude, can it. I don't need you to talk me up."

"I wasn't. I was talking about me." Jason stood with a smile and flashed her a wink. "You going to introduce me to the lady, or should I do it myself over drinks after her shift?"

Tony cut him a warning look—the dudes' equivalent of *back off, bitch, he's mine*—even though he knew Jason wasn't serious. "J, this is one of my oldest friends Trish. Trish, this is one of my newer—and as of yet, still in a trial period—friends, Jason. He moved to town a few years ago as the new gym teacher at the middle school."

"Pleased to meet you, Jason." She held her hand out for a shake, but Jason turned it and kissed the top of her hand in what Tony assumed was the cheesiest greeting ever to happen in a Midwestern Irish pub.

"Pleasure's mine, Trish. But I'd be happy to make it yours."

Bastard. "Did I mention the trial period, asshole?" Tony asked wryly.

Jason chuckled just as Erin swooped in and looped her arm through his. "Trish, you're due for your break, and I'm not letting you skip it again. Jason used to work here so he'll help me up at the bar, won't you, stud?"

"Flattery will get you everywhere, sweetheart," Jason said before kissing her on the cheek. "Besides, if I stick around, poor Tony won't stand a chance with your lovely new bartender. Lead the way."

Once Jason was gone, Tony took his first deep breath since turning to see Trish standing in front of him. He'd have to remember to thank Erin later. And backhand Jason in his nuts. On second thought, he and Erin should be square now. She owed him for not telling him who the "new girl" was when she knew damn well it'd trip him up.

Apparently matchmaker and troublemaker were interchangeable.

"Sorry if Jason embarrassed you or anything," he said. "He's a tool sometimes, but totally harmless."

She let out a light laugh. "Yeah, I gathered that pretty quickly. Don't worry, I won't hold your friendship against you."

"Thanks." They both stared at each other, smiling. It'd felt great joking around and laughing with her like the old days, but the reality of her being in Fort—instead of in her fancy life in New York—had finally sunk in, and he didn't feel much like laughing anymore. "Damn, it's good to see you, gorgeous."

"You know, I used to get hugs with your hellos." She canted her head, her long brown hair falling to one side, and the corners of her lips twitched. "Will the other kids on the playground make fun of you for hugging a girl?"

"Nah." He pulled her in and folded her into his arms. The feel of her cheek pressed against his chest sent his heart into overdrive. He hoped she didn't notice. "I'm king of the playground now. Anyone makes fun of me and they get kicked off the monkey bars."

"Impressive. I'm glad I hold favor with the king, then. The monkey bars were always my favorite."

"Mine too. Especially when the girls wore dresses."

Predictably, she laughed and tried to pull away, but he wasn't letting her go that easily. Laughing, he made the expected feigned apologies and held her tight for as long as she'd let him. Resting his chin on top of her head, he inhaled the sweet jasmine scent— the one he couldn't place earlier—of her favorite lotion. It brought back so many memories. Ones he hadn't thought about in years.

As close friends, he'd held her on multiple occasions, and hugging hello and goodbye was second nature for them. He'd always wanted more than those platonic affections, but back in their school days Tony never allowed himself to think it'd ever be possible.

But the last time she'd come home to visit—five whole years ago—he'd started to think "what if." He'd grown well into his body by then, and while he wasn't as muscular as he was now, he'd still been toned and fit. That alone gave him confidence with women he hadn't had before.

The last night they spent time together before she headed back to New York, she'd been tucked into his arms, her cheek resting against his chest as they watched a movie. And that's when the "what ifs" crept in. *What if* he tipped her chin up, lowered his mouth to hers, and kissed her until they couldn't breathe? *What if* he pulled her onto his lap, cupped her ass with his large hands, and caused her nipples to pebble against his chest...

But by then, Trish was four years into a relationship with some Nick asshole who could never bother himself to fly home with her. Trish had chosen to be with another man, and he couldn't do anything more than suck it up and keep his *what ifs* to his damn self. Tony almost snorted. She hadn't *chosen* anyone over him; he'd never had the balls to make himself an option for her. So as much as he'd wanted her that night on his couch, Tony wouldn't betray her trust by pushing the boundaries of their friendship.

Fuck, he'd gone to sleep later still fantasizing about sinking himself between her thighs and feeling her insides squeeze his cock so tight it was painful. When he woke up the next morning, he realized the pain was real. He'd been so hard all damn night that his dick felt like it would explode from the sheet dragging over it. It took three times of jerking off in the shower before he could leave the house without being arrested for public indecency.

Trish broke through his trip down Fucked Up Lane when she pulled away and took a seat in Jason's empty chair. He sat, too, suddenly holding a grudge against the table separating them. Jesus fucking Christ, he needed to get a grip.

"So, you finally left the Big Apple to sit on your rightful throne as queen of our quaint little town?"

She rolled her eyes. "Hardly. I mean, I did leave New York, but I'm only staying here for a couple of months or so."

Tony was careful not to let his disappointment show. Mainly because it pissed him off. It shouldn't bother him that she planned to leave again. At least not to the degree that it did. "What happens in a couple of months?" *And what happened to whats-his-nuts?*

"A good friend of mine is opening up a dress shop in Chicago and asked if I wanted to go in as partners." Trish shrugged. "I haven't decided if that's what I want to do yet, but as soon as I get some things figured out, I'm out of here."

"Still not a huge fan of small town life, I see."

She offered him a wan smile. "Afraid not."

They talked for another ten minutes or so about inane shit. Anything considered polite conversation and nothing overly personal, like what happened between her and the guy she'd been in love with. He was simultaneously pissed and relieved that she didn't talk to him about it. How was that for indecisive?

Catching her gaze on the beer he'd finished during their talk, she said, "I'd better get back to work. It's been great talking to you, Tony. I'll have Jason bring you back another beer."

She grabbed the empty bottle just as he did the same thing. Trish pointedly glanced at his hand now wrapped around hers, then back up at him with a look in her eyes he couldn't read.

Reluctantly, he pulled his hand away, and she quickly pushed up to her feet to head back to the bar. *Say something, dumbass, don't let this be it. Say something!* "Trish, wait."

She turned back. "Yes?"

Tony stood and gave her a confident smile he didn't fully feel. "I'd love to take you out sometime and catch up some more. It's been too long."

A hint of anxiety flickered across her face as she dropped her gaze to the bottle in her hands. Probably worried he'd dig into why she was back. "Hey," he said and waited for her to meet his eyes. "It's okay. We don't have to talk if you don't want. We can just enjoy each other and have a good time." As soon as the words left his mouth, Tony winced. "Sorry. That sounded a lot different in my head. I swear it's not a sleazy proposition." Trying to lighten the mood, he added, "Unless you want it to be, in which case I totally meant it to sound like that."

She rolled her eyes and playfully slapped his chest. He dutifully rubbed the area as though she'd hurt him. "Yeah, okay, I'd like that. Not the sleazy proposition," she said with a healthy dose of stink eye thrown his way, "but going out would be a nice change from holing up at Rhi's house all the time."

"Great. I'll pick you up tomorrow morning at ten o'clock." Tony barely stopped himself from an embarrassing victory fist pump. Unfortunately, he had no control over the goofy grin making his cheeks hurt. "And make sure you're hungry."

CHAPTER TWO

Tony knocked on Trish's sister's door the next morning and waited with his hands shoved in his jeans pockets. He wasn't nervous, but he wasn't as confident as he normally was either. Trish was the only girl who had ever made him feel like this, and he hated it.

The door opened and Rhianna stood on the other side, staring at him through the screen door. "Well, well, look what the cat dragged in. Tony DiAngelo. How ya doin'? Been to the pool recently?"

Tony grinned at the woman who threatened him on a regular basis as kids. She was six years older than Trish and had worked as a lifeguard at the aquatic center. Since Tony was one of the "pool rats"—the name the lifeguards gave to the kids with season passes who spent every day in the water—it was easy for Rhianna to tease him mercilessly about his relationship with her baby sister. If she felt particularly feisty, she'd toss in a threat or two of bodily harm. It was all in good fun, though. At least, he'd hoped it was.

"Hi, Rhianna. Can't say that I've been since I stopped life-guarding myself. You?"

"Not since the kids were little. Now they're old enough to go on their own, thank God."

Tony laughed. "So now *your* kids are the pool rats, huh? Strange how life comes full circle."

Rhianna smiled and pushed the screen door open, stepping aside to let him in. "Incredibly strange. So, you putting the moves on my sister while she's in town?"

Tony crossed the threshold and stood his ground just inside. "No need to break out your torture implements. We're just going to breakfast."

Cocking her head, she studied him. Then proceeded to shock the hell out of him. "That's too bad. I'd actually encourage it this time. Either way, getting out of the house will be good for her."

He heard someone descending the stairs and looked up to see Trish dressed in black tights, a black lightweight sweater that ended at mid-thigh, and a wide red belt that made it look like a dress. Or maybe it was a dress that looked like a belted sweater? Her makeup was done, earrings dangled long and played peek-aboo from under her dark curls. She was dressed to go out to a club or fancy restaurant.

"I think that's the pot calling the kettle black, Rhi," Trish said as she reached the bottom. "I'm pretty sure you qualify for hermit status. You're practically agoraphobic."

"Why would I want to leave the comfort of my own home when I have everything I need here?"

Trish slipped on a pair of black ankle boots. "Yeah, okay, well let's remember to mind our own business, hmm?"

In a mock patronizing tone, Rhi patted Trish on the head and said, "Oh, sweetie, but you *are* my business. Now go have fun before I lock you out of the house and force you to stay with mom."

Trish narrowed her eyes. "You wouldn't."

"Try me," Rhi answered with an evil grin.

Tony used that as his cue and placed a hand on Trish's lower back to usher her out. "Come on, Trish. I've found a fast retreat is best when she starts slinging threats."

Trish snorted and let him guide her onto the porch, but called over her shoulder so her sister would hear her loud and clear. "Don't worry, the lion with the loudest roar is always the biggest pussy."

They heard Rhi laugh as she closed the door behind them and Trish smiled at Tony, making his chest a little tighter. When they reached his car, she stopped. "Um, Tony?"

He followed her gaze to his door. "Shit. I forgot about that." The door was dented in the middle making the seam next to the front quarter panel stick out so far he could see the hinges. "Mrs. Danvers t-boned me last night going through The Intersection."

The Intersection was what the townies called the only road crossing with an actual stoplight on Main Street. Trish's eyes widened. "You mean our old English teacher, Mrs. Danvers? How is that woman even still alive? I swear she was in her eighties when she taught us in seventh grade. No way she should be driving."

"Yeah, well, I don't know if you can call it driving. The cop estimated her speed at no more than ten miles an hour." He stared at the twisted metal panel in disgust. "Just enough to screw up my door, but not nearly enough to do me the favor of totaling it out."

"How much will it cost to fix?"

"More than it will to get another door from the junkyard and give it to the high school tech ed class to install as part of their final exam. But that's a few weeks away, so I'm stuck with it until then." Testing the door handle, he tugged on it a little, then decided to leave well enough alone. Better that it was stuck closed than open and unable to latch. "Would you be okay with climbing over from my side? Or you can sit in back and I'll be your friendly neighborhood chauffeur service."

She laughed as they walked around and he opened his door

for her. "I think I can manage," she said, ducking into the car to start her crawl to the other side. "I won't make you service me today."

No sooner had the words left her mouth when she froze in place, hands on the seat, and her perfectly rounded ass poised in front of him. "Okay, that is so not what I meant to say."

Bracing his forearms on the edge of the roof, he leaned in and used his bedroom voice. "You sure, T? Maybe you'd like to pick a different day to make me *service* you."

Her head turned to look at him over her shoulder with wide eyes and her lips parted. He fisted his hands to keep them from reaching for her ass and pulling it back against his hardening cock. The thought of seeing her in this position in his bed, back arched and begging him for more... *Fuck fuck fuck.*

Tony knew he had to erase the innuendo—make it into a joke to wipe it off their slate, just as he'd always done—if he wanted to keep her friendship and spend time with her. And given the choice, he'd always want her in his life as something, rather than nothing.

"Still so easy to tease." Grinning wide, he winked at her. "Thought the big city life would have toughened you up. It's nice to see I was wrong."

She gave him a dramatic harrumph and finally settled into the passenger seat. They buckled up and he turned the car toward the bypass highway. "You look beautiful, by the way," Tony said, glancing at her briefly before returning his attention back to the road.

"Thanks, you do too. I mean, not *beautiful*, but you know. Like, buff and stuff." Tony hitched a brow in her direction and tried to keep the amusement from his face. Unsuccessfully. Her cheeks filled with a dusky rose color as she cleared her throat and predictably changed topics. "So, where are we going?"

"I thought since you've been gone so long it's probably been a while since you've had a cream puff as big as your head."

She gasped and without looking, he could hear her wide smile when she spoke. "Pine Cone."

"Pine Cone," he said with a nod. "Hope you're hungry and ready for a massive sugar high."

"Absofuckinglutely."

Woman after his own heart.

TRISH COULDN'T REMEMBER the last time she'd gone to Pine Cone. It was a truck stop restaurant about fifteen minutes away with great food for cheap prices. But they were famous for their cream puffs and chocolate éclairs as big as your face. Literally. They were so damn good.

Trish walked through the door that Tony held for her—something Nick had never made a point to do—and waited at the hostess podium to be seated as the "sign" crafted with notebook paper and a Sharpie instructed. Tony stood next to her, looking over a menu.

Trish had spent the entire car ride studying him from the corner of her eye. She couldn't get over how much different he looked from the friend in all her graduation pictures. He'd still had a boyish appearance about him back then. But the next time she saw him, he'd grown several inches and left all boyish traces behind. That had been shocking enough on its own, and now he'd bulked up—big time—so that he almost looked like an entirely different person.

No, that wasn't true. It was still clearly him. He had the same hooded eyes that saw more than they should. The same smile she found comfort in, no matter what was happening in her life. Between his body finally getting the Time to Grow memo and whatever he did to pack on the muscle, the finished result looked damn good on him.

As did the faded jeans that hugged his ass and his concert T-shirt that pulled nicely over his chest and stretched from his biceps when he bent his arms. His coloring was a palette of browns, which sounded like a description for an ugly tweed jacket from the seventies, but looked delicious on him. She and Tony were both Italian, but him more so than her, and it showed. His hair was medium brown and curled a bit at the ends from being too long. The color of his eyes reminded her of hazelnuts, and his skin was already tan from playing baseball and soccer.

Yeah, okay, she *may* have done some social media stalking after she got home last night. But is it really stalking when people post it for all the world to see? She liked to think not. Besides, she had a lot of catching up to do on the goings-on of her old friends. When she started dating Nick, her Facebook days slowly diminished over time until she eventually stopped checking her account. He hated social media and said it was a waste of time. But then, anyone he ever knew or cared about still lived in the same neighborhood with them, so he didn't have a need for it.

Tony didn't appear to use his account much, but his mom and sisters tagged him in a ton of pictures. His timeline was one big scrapbook of his life, told through the lenses of others' cameras. Everything from him playing soccer and baseball, to coaching little kids, to playing with his nieces and nephews.

The latter ones in particular had tugged on her heart a little too hard for her liking. Her biological clock had been sounding a lot more like a ticking bomb for the last couple of years, but Nick promised they'd have kids as soon as they moved out of the city. Too bad she didn't know at the time that he had no intentions of moving, making kids a moot point.

At thirty years old, almost all of her friends had gotten married and started families years ago. It made Trish feel like an old spinster who should hit up the local animal shelters to start obtaining members for her future horde of cats. And wasn't that the most pathetic thing ever.

Finally, the hostess led them through the restaurant, and

somewhere in the world a record must have scratched. Every customer in the place stared openly at her as she walked by. But they weren't meeting her eyes; their focus was on the rest of her body. Her clothes? She hadn't worn anything racy, and without checking, she was fairly certain she hadn't strapped her bra on the outside of her sweater dress. She felt like one of those celebrities on the red carpet who had unfortunate wardrobe malfunctions and ended up on *TMZ*.

As they slipped into the booth in the back of the restaurant Tony smiled and said, "You sure know how to make an entrance."

"Yeah, what the heck is up with that?" she asked in a hushed voice. "Do I have toilet paper hanging out of my leggings or something?"

"You really don't know?"

Her brow furrowed in response. She hadn't a clue.

"Okay, but don't take offense."

"When someone says that it's because the other person is guaranteed to take offense," she said wryly.

"Seriously, it's not bad. It's just that you look...different."

"I haven't even changed my hair in years. Plus, none of these people know me."

"No, not different from before." He nodded slightly to the dining area, indicating the customers. "Different from them." Then he peered down at his shirt and plucked at the material. "From us."

"Wait, are you saying they're staring at me because I'm not in a pair of old jeans and a T-shirt?" He shrugged as though to say *what else did you expect*? "What's wrong with what I'm wearing?"

"There's nothing wrong with what you're wearing. You look amazing, Trish." His eyes warmed her from the inside, and the tiny lift at one corner of his mouth didn't hurt either. "You just went and got citified on us, that's all."

"What-a-fied?"

"Citified. You adapted to the ways of the big city."

"That's not a thing."

He arched a brow. "Looks like it is from where I'm sitting."

"I suppose in a month when it's hot and humid I'll be expected to wear Daisy Dukes and a plaid shirt knotted between my boobs."

Tony's face turned stone serious. "Dear God, I hope so. Tell me what I have to do make that happen."

Trish faked a disgusted sound and threw a few sweetener packets at him. He laughed, blocking his face from the sugar shrapnel. The waitress showed up with coffee and took their orders. As soon as she left, he started arranging their forks and knives in the middle of the table into what the newest generation called a hashtag, and a wave of giddy nostalgia swept over her.

"Oh my God, I don't think I've done this since high school," she said, gathering half a dozen pink Sweet-N-Low packets then handing him a few more of the white sugar packets to add to the ones he'd recovered from her attack. She placed one of her packets in a corner space.

He set a white packet in the center spot. He clearly hadn't gotten any better at Table Tic-Tac-Toe. "How else did you pass the time in a restaurant?"

She thought about that for a moment and almost didn't tell him. Now that she was on the outside looking in, she recognized how disconnected her life had been the past decade. For a city of eight million people, New Yorkers were incredibly isolated people. No one made eye contact while walking down the street or struck up a conversation with the person next to them on the subway. More often than not, they had their heads bowed, looking down at their phones, a book, or newspaper. Trish could describe the people she saw every day during her commute to work by their hair color, a favorite hat, or coat during the cold months. But she rarely saw their faces.

Trish shrugged and placed another marker. "Not with anything as fun as beating you at Table Tic-Tac-Toe."

"You know I let you win, right?"

"Whatever gets you through the night, DiAngelo."

He chuckled. "Nice to see you and Rhi are still as feisty as ever together."

"Yeah, we're still really close. I don't know what I would've done if she hadn't insisted I move in with her for a while." Trish lifted her coffee with both hands and sipped, reveling in the bold strength meant to help truckers stay awake at all hours of the night. It wasn't for delicate palettes, that was for sure.

"You can't stay with your mom?"

She clapped a hand over her mouth to stifle the laugh trying to shoot coffee out her nose. After carefully swallowing, she said, "I could, but we wouldn't last more than a few days before driving each other insane. I love my mom, and it's been nice being able to see her whenever I want these last few weeks, but we do best in small doses together."

"I guess some things never change, then," he said with a smile.

"No, I guess they don't."

They continued to play their game—Trish won three times out of five—and caught up on the goings on in each other's lives. Everything that didn't have to do with relationships, anyway. They shared stories about their families, jobs, and friends, pausing when their massive cream puffs arrived so they could moan around their first bite of pastry heaven.

Okay, so she was the only one who closed her eyes and moaned like a woman starved. When she came out of her mini-foodgasm a few seconds later, Tony and a few of the men at surrounding tables were frozen in various stages of eating, staring at her like she'd just flashed them her boobs. She felt the flush of embarrassment ride all the way to her hairline and cleared her throat awkwardly before taking a long sip of her water. Thankfully, the men had recovered and went about their business by the time she set her glass down.

All except Tony whose heated gaze held her in place with an unseen force she couldn't explain. She'd never seen him look like this before. Like a deadly cat, hunting his prey and content to stalk it for however long it took, to strike only when she would be at her weakest.

Then, as quickly as it flashed over his face, it was gone in the next instant, replaced by his charming smile and reassuring wink like she'd imagined the whole thing. When nothing like it happened again for the duration of their breakfast date, she decided her mind had played a trick on her. Whether it was a hallucination from the massive sugar rush or her desperation to have a man see her as desirable for the first time in years, she didn't know. Nor did it matter. The last thing she needed was to get involved with anyone, much less someone from her hometown.

But Tony's friendship was comforting and kept her mind off things she'd rather not think about. So until she left again, she'd enjoy that whenever he offered, and she hoped he offered often.

CHAPTER THREE

I t'd been a few weeks of spending time with Trish. School was out, which meant Tony now had a lot of free time, so whenever their schedules allowed, they found something to do together. They went for runs almost every morning. She dragged him against his will to the mall. He retaliated and made her go fishing. They met for coffee, went to the movies, and took her sister's boxer puppy to the dog park.

It felt like how they were in high school.

At the same time, it felt nothing like that.

Tony told himself over and over again that he was imagining things. That her lingering touches weren't very lingering at all. That the way she sometimes peered up at him through her impossibly long lashes with a half-grin didn't mean she was wondering *what if* or *what would it be like*. That the times he caught her staring at his mouth didn't mean she wanted him to kiss the living hell out of her.

Yeah, he told himself all that. And then the devil on his shoulder—also known as his dick and was nowhere near his shoulder—reminded him he wasn't an inexperienced kid misreading signs. Whether she knew it or not, on some level,

Trish wanted something more with him. How *much* more, he couldn't say.

Maybe just some kissing.

Maybe kissing and heavy groping.

Maybe, just maybe, she wanted everything.

It was that infinitesimal possibility that made him hard more often than not. He wondered if he should seek medical help if his erection lasted longer than four hours even if he'd never taken any pills. It couldn't be healthy. It sure as fuck wasn't comfortable.

But no matter how much he thought she might want more or he ended up with a perpetual state of blue balls, Tony wouldn't be the one to make the first move. Not because he was unsure of himself or his seduction skills. If Trish were any other girl, he would've made his move the first time he caught the hint of her interest. He'd rather get rejected than not try, though he couldn't think of a time where that'd happened. Not because he was God's gift to women, but because he wasn't a douchebag who initiated things where they weren't welcome.

But Trish was different. He cared a hell of a lot about this woman, and she was still fresh off a bad break up he knew nothing about. No way was he going to ruin what he had with her over an unwanted kiss. Having her as a friend was better than nothing at all. So if she wanted something more, she'd have to at least give him a crystal clear signal.

Tonight, he'd brought her to the old drive-in. It always showed a double feature and had been a favorite place of theirs to go over the years. He borrowed his dad's pickup truck and parked facing backward in the grass lot. After making a cozy lounging area with a few thick comforters, they propped themselves up with several pillows and laid side by side in the bed of the truck.

It was early June and the perfect time of year for the outdoor theater. When the weather was still decently warm at night, but not too buggy where they had to douse themselves in disgusting sprays. The cloudless night sky was an endless blanket of stars that they'd studied and pointed out constellations in before the first movie began.

The first movie had been a comedy, one they'd both wanted to see and laughed so hard that their sides hurt. The second was some kind of drama neither had heard of. Since there were no jokes or high-speed chases or massive explosions, Tony didn't deem it worth his attention.

He'd rather watch her watch the movie. And, yes, he realized how creepy that sounded in his head, but the reality wasn't that bad. From her vantage point—her head resting where his shoulder met his chest—she'd have to twist around to even see his face. So he studied her absently and systematically pick at the polish on her finger nails. Saw her bare feet rocking on her heels like metronomes until something in the movie made her tense up and she curled her toes in tight. And he especially loved watching the different emotions play out on her face.

"Ugh, such a typical man thing to do," she said to the jumbo-gigantic screen. "What an asshole."

"As a man, I should probably ask for clarification so I can defend my gender."

"Aren't you watching?"

Oh, I'm watching. Just not the same thing you are. "Must have zoned out. Fill me in."

"He's breaking up with her because he doesn't think he's good enough for her. But instead of being honest and telling her that, he says shit to hurt her so she won't want to be with him."

She sounded like it hit a little too close to home. Tony wondered what exactly her ex said to her when they broke things off. Did he do the same thing or was it just seeing any kind of break up that set her on edge?

He wanted her to talk to him about it. He wanted to know how the prick hurt her, but he also wanted her to get it out. According to Rhianna and Erin, Trish never talked about it and changed the subject if they brought it up. She was letting it eat at her from the inside, and the longer she waited to purge that shit, the harder it'd be to get rid of.

Tony thought about how to respond. Maybe play devil's advocate and see what happens. "He thinks he's being noble by sacrificing what he wants for what's best for her. He only wants her to be happy."

Trish turned onto her side and held herself up on her forearm. "Bullshit."

In the dark, he made out her narrowed eyes and tense jaw. Things he wanted to soothe into relaxed states with feather-light kisses. But he wouldn't. He couldn't. Not yet. Maybe not ever.

"Okay," he said. "State your case."

"If he truly wanted her happy, then he'd go to her with his worries and insecurities and talk it out like adults. And maybe when it's all said and done, maybe she *does* decide that it won't or can't work between them, but at least he let her make her own decision. Why do men think they have the right to make decisions for us? Do you truly see us as such feebleminded creatures that we couldn't possibly know our own minds, our needs, our desires? I mean, how fucking arrogant can you be? It's not only high-handed, it's *downright insulting*."

Sparks lit up her eyes, and although her rant ended up including him—accusing him—he knew he wasn't the one she was truly mad at.

"Is that what he did, sweetheart?" he asked softly.

She winced and suddenly found great interest in a loose thread on the blanket under them. Tony lifted his right hand and tucked her hair behind her ear, letting his fingers trail the edge of her jaw before tipping her chin up to meet his gaze. "Did he end things and say it was for your benefit?"

Tears gathered in the water line of her eyes. "I don't want to talk about it."

Hatred for the man he'd never met slithered in his gut. He had to consciously keep his hands from balling into fists that ached to physically hurt Nick as much as he'd mentally hurt Trish emotionally. But Tony wouldn't get that chance, and even if he did, it'd only make *him* feel better to make the bastard pay for shattering her heart. The one thing Nick should have protected at all costs.

But he didn't, and now Trish was in Tony's arms, and he'd let her stay in them for as long as she wanted.

"Then we won't talk about it." Tony gathered her closer, situating her back into their movie-lounging position, and kissed her hairline by her temple as though sealing the lid on the topic.

Her right arm rested along his left side. Turning it so the underside faced up, he ran the tips of his fingers up and down the length in slow, soothing trails. Minutes later, she surprised him by speaking.

"We were supposed to get married. Move out of the city, away from his overbearing family. Have kids." She paused. "Well, I wanted kids. He always pushed the topic off, saying we should only work on one part of our lives at a time. In hindsight, I don't think he ever wanted them. At least not with me."

Tony had a hundred things he wanted to say. *He was a fool. He didn't have any idea how special you are. In a hundred years, a guy like him could never be good enough for you. You deserve so much more.*

Instead, he kept quiet. She wouldn't be receptive to any of that now, and it's probably nothing she hasn't heard over and over again from her family and friends. At this point, it was just noise. So he gave her arm a light squeeze to let her know he was still listening, still there for her, and continued running his fingers over her satiny skin.

"Then out of nowhere, he sits me down and tells me he decided he can't bring himself to move out of the city. And not only the city, but he doesn't want to move away from his *neighborhood*. The one he'd lived in his entire life. The one where his parents lived across the street from us in the same apartment he'd been raised in. I'd lived across the country from my family from the time I was eighteen, and at almost forty years old, he couldn't move one goddamn hour away from his.

"And when I got upset—rightly so, I might add, since we'd been planning this future together for several years at this point —he used it against me, saying things like, 'See? I'm only holding you back from what you really want. I'm not good enough for you.'"

Again, she turned into him and raised up on her elbow so her face was level with his.

"But do you know what that really means?" she continued. "It really means that *I* wasn't good enough for *him*." Tony opened his mouth to reprimand her for even letting the thought cross her mind, but she kept going. "Because if I was, he would have been willing to at least compromise on things. Meet me halfway or *part*way or *some* fucking way. But I wasn't good enough or important enough...not loved enough."

The sparks were gone, replaced by pools of hurt lit by the moon. It killed him that he couldn't take the hurt away for her.

"Jesus, come here." He pulled her in, tucking her face into his neck and holding her tight. Warm tears streamed down his throat and dampened the collar of his T-shirt. He hated that she was crying. Even worse that she was crying over someone who cast her aside like an old pair of shoes that outgrew their purpose. *Fucking asshole.* "You're right. About him not loving you enough. But it's because he loves himself so goddamn much that he can't see past his own ego long enough to know how lucky he was to have such an amazing woman. His shortcomings are *not* a reflection of you. They only prove he's a selfish bastard who didn't deserve you or your love."

She sniffled. "I know. I mean, I know that now. I've been doing a lot of thinking." An angry curse whispered across his neck. "Hell, that's all I've been doing for the last month. And I finally realized that what hurts me the most is that his bullshit excuses about holding me back and not being good enough for me are dead on...and I wasted all those years because I couldn't see that his love wasn't real, that *none* of it was real.

"I'm not upset that our relationship ended. I'm upset at the thought of what those wasted years could have been if I'd had the good sense to end it myself. And I'm scared that I'll make the same mistake. That I'll start building a life with someone only to find out later that I was wrong about him, too. I don't trust myself when it comes to relationships anymore."

Tony sighed and held her tighter. "No one knows if the person they're with will end up being the right one. It's still a gamble for even the happiest of couples. The best you can do is place your bet when the odds are most in your favor."

"Yeah," she said. "I guess so."

"Either way, it's not something you should be stressing about right now. You need to give yourself permission to take the time to figure out what it is you want to do from here."

Trish tucked her feet back and pushed up to sit on them. "You're right. I need to stop obsessing over the past and even the future. To stop thinking about this shit day in and day out. I'm so damn tired of thinking, Tony."

"I'm not surprised." He pushed up to a sitting position, right knee bent with his arm resting on top. "So then give yourself a break. Whether your plan is to stick around for another month or another year. I vote for the latter, by the way."

Finally, she smiled. Not the kind that stretched wide and accompanied laughter. But the soft kind that followed an exhausting bout of sadness. Trails of moisture still shone on her cheeks. He felt compelled to remove any evidence of her pain. He lifted his right hand and used the backs of his fingers to wipe them away. "There," he said. "Now there's nothing left of your past to hold you down. From this moment on, you're going to live in the moment."

"You've always been good at the carefree thing." Her gaze dropped to his mouth and held. He felt the weight of it sink into his lips and race down into his cock. Jesus Christ, she had no idea what she was doing to him. "Tony?"

"Yeah?"

She lifted her eyes to his again and then dragged her bottom lip through her teeth. It wasn't a gesture of seduction, but one of insecurity. "Will you help me live in the moment?"

In the background, the characters in the movie were still playing out their story. Every so often, murmurs of people talking or ordering from concessions mixed in, a good reminder of where they were and that they weren't alone. But all he heard was the beat of his own heart and the blood rushing in his ears.

Without thinking, he slid his hand through her hair to cradle the back of her head and brought his mouth down on hers in a soul-crushing kiss. For years he'd imagined what a first kiss would be like between them. Soft and tender, slow as they explored one another. But anyone who lusted after someone for most of their life should come with a warning label that read "Contents under pressure. Do not puncture." Because the moment Trish's gaze settled on his mouth, she split him wide open, causing him to explode.

He couldn't think beyond each second that passed, afraid that if he started hoping for more Karma would pay him a visit and rip it all away for being greedy. But when she fisted the front of his shirt and melted into him on a barely audible whimper, Tony changed tactics. To hell with the consequences. If this was the only time he'd have her like this, he would damn sure take all he could get.

Wrapping his arms around her waist, he hauled her onto his lap to straddle him. Since she'd come home, her wardrobe relaxed a little at a time; becoming less city and more country. She still liked her skirts, though, which he was currently thankful as hell for. Her short jean skirt bunched at the top of her thighs to allow her legs to part this wide. And that left only her panties as a barrier between him and her humid sex.

She kept herself a little farther back from where he'd like, but he wouldn't rush her. Refocusing his energy back to her mouth, he grabbed a fistful of her hair and angled her head, then licked the length of her lips. She opened on a sigh, giving him access to the sweetest thing he'd ever tasted.

His tongue swept in and danced with hers at the edges of his control. He groaned. She moaned. He grabbed her by her ass and squeezed, his fingertips running along the edges of her panties, conjuring wicked thoughts flashing through his mind like a synaptic seizure.

Then she gave him a game changer. With two tiny forward movements on her knees, she centered herself directly over his cock...then lowered and rocked her hips forward to drag her hot sex back and forth.

It was Heaven.

It was Hell.

Though it nearly killed him, Tony wrenched his mouth away and pressed his forehead to hers, the sound of his breaths sawing in and out of his lungs a testament to how far gone this girl made him in such a short amount of time. "Hold on, T. I need to be sure this is okay with you. That I'm not taking advantage of a situation where you're not thinking clearly."

"My thoughts have never been clearer. I want this. I might even need it. I want to lose myself with you. I want you to make it so I can't think, only feel. No strings and no expectations."

It stung that she felt the need to draw lines in the sand. Set parameters for their time together. Even though he knew this was nothing more than an arrangement between them, he hated feeling like they were at a conference table discussing terms. But now wasn't the time to let his pride get in the way. She was offering him exactly what he wanted. A chance to be with her, to finally know what it's like to have her in every way possible. He knew this is all it could be for now. She was eventually leaving for another city and nowhere in this conversation had she offered for him to leave with her.

"Don't worry, in a few weeks I'll be gone again and you'll be off the hook," she said with a hesitant smile.

Ouch.

Injecting levity at the end was her way of dealing with things when she was nervous. But he wasn't in the mood to laugh, and no doubt his face showed it. He watched as her sweet smile melted away, leaving her lower lip a prisoner of her front teeth.

"Anthony...?"

She only used his proper name for serious conversations. Or if he was in trouble, but then she tacked on his middle name too.

Jesus, what the hell was his problem? He should be jumping all over this, but somehow it felt...off. It didn't make sense. If Jason were here, he'd smack the back of Tony's head and tell him to quit being such a pussy.

Trish knelt up to move from his lap, shaking her head. "I'm sorry, I shouldn't have asked that. Forget I said—"

Fuck that. He banded one arm around her lower back and dragged her back in, then gripped the side of her head and shut her up with a searing kiss. She went stiff at first, but as he moved his mouth over hers, she melded into his body from hips to chest. He grunted when she rocked herself against the length of his cock straining against his fly.

He'd never been so fucking hard in his life. With every forward motion, she killed him a little more, bit by bit tipping the scales from pleasure to pain as he tried to keep from coming in his jeans. But he'd gladly suffer ten times over as long as it made her feel good and got her off. If her reactions right now were anything to go by, he'd say she was fast on her way.

Her pace steadily increased and the fingers fisted in his hair pulled harder. His hands lowered to her ass and squeezed in encouragement, sensing she needed this more than he understood, and he wanted nothing more than to give it to her.

A loud thud and laughter came from a couple cars down and brought the world around them back into focus. Trish buried her face on his chest and held still in his arms.

"My God, woman, you made me lose my damn head." No matter how badly he wanted to burrow beneath the blankets and take her right then, he refused to let their first time together be like a couple of teenagers pretending to watch a movie when the parents were home. "In the truck. I'm inviting you back to my place and you're accepting."

Tony picked her up by her waist and set her off to the side, and then scooped up all the blankets in one jumbled pile before jumping over the side of the truck.

"Assumptions and high-handed commands tend to piss me off," she said.

Shoving everything in the back seat of the cab, he slammed the door and turned just as she dropped down next to him. "Sweetheart, we can have angry sex if you want, as long as the end result is me sinking deep inside you and making you come so hard you forget your own name." He gave her a crooked smirk.

A few seconds passed as she studied him wide-eyed as though his words were taking their sweet time sinking in. Finally she snapped out of it with a hard blink and cleared her throat. "I guess I can live with that."

"Good. Now hop in and buckle up. I plan on breaking some traffic laws."

CHAPTER FOUR

T rish watched the world pass in a blur from the passenger seat as Tony drove them the ten minutes back to his house. The music wasn't blaring, but just loud enough to make conversation difficult, which was fine with her because anything she said at this point would sound like some cheesy attempt to ignore the we're-about-to-cross-*that*-line elephant sitting squarely between them. Awkward silence was the next best thing, she supposed.

It's not that she didn't want to follow through on what she asked him. When Tony kissed her that first time, she'd been flooded with things she couldn't remember feeling with Nick. They'd been together so long that the excitement and passion they'd shared in the beginning of their relationship got buried under years and years of routine and comfortable compatibility.

But Tony's kiss... Her cheeks flushed and she reached up to touch her fingertips to her lips. She'd felt like a spring of cool water for his desert-dry mouth. Needed with a desperation she didn't understand and yet didn't want to waste time thinking about it. Instead, she gave herself over to the sensations washing over her and let her body take control.

And holy shit did it ever. She'd never felt like that before, like she was acting on pure instinct. She'd rubbed herself on him like an alley cat in heat. In the middle of the outdoor theater, no less. If she wasn't already at the center of the gossip mill, having public sex would have done the trick. Thank God for the drunk idiot who fell out of his car and gave them a much needed reality check.

No, the awkward silence now came from being nervous. Like, really, *really* nervous. In the heat of the moment, she wasn't focusing on how out of practice she was in the sexual department. Or that the practice she *did* have probably wasn't worth much anyway. But now that the haze of desire had burned off, every insecurity she had about her sexual prowess—or lack thereof—ran in random zigzag patterns in her brain, crashing into each other and slamming against the edges of her worst dating fear. To make matters worse, there was one thing in particular she had to tell him before they got too far into things, and it could be a huge buzzkill.

Trish was so caught up in her thoughts that she didn't realize they arrived until she felt Tony throw the truck in park and kill the engine. She looked over at him. Unsure what to do with her hands, she kept them in her lap and kept her fingers busy with each other as though they had an actual purpose for being there. *Tell him tell him tell him.*

Stretching his right arm along the back of the bench seat, Tony turned to face her...and then waited. Why was he waiting? Did he change his mind? Maybe he preferred aggressive women. But even if she wanted to be the aggressor, she wouldn't have the slightest idea how to go about it, and even if she did, she'd feel stupid instead of sexy. *Shit.*

"You're nervous." He always could read her better than anyone. Denying his statement would be futile. "It's just me, T. I'd never do anything you're uncomfortable with."

"If there's any man I trust implicitly in this world, Tony,

it's you."

"Good. Then why the nerves?"

Oh, God. The space in the cab shrunk around her and the air grew thick. She did not want to have this conversation with him. But Tony was like a shark if he sniffed even a drop of blood in the water. He'd pursue relentlessly until he got what he wanted, which in this case, was a truthful answer.

"I realize this isn't the best thing to say to get in the mood, and I'll totally understand if you think it kills the moment, but I feel it's something you should know beforehand."

Tony narrowed his eyes. "Did that asshole give you an STD?"

"What? God no, Tony, it's nothing like that."

He gave her a curt nod. "Okay, I'm listening."

"You just need to know that it's not because of something you do or don't do—"

"Trish, you're rambling. What's the 'it' in that statement?"

She released a heavy sigh and forced herself to spit it out. "My inability to orgasm."

If he'd forgotten his contacts while sitting in on a lecture from someone with a thick accent, this is what he would look like. She almost laughed. Dear lord, even confused and squinty-eyed the man was still handsome.

"I'm not following," he said. "Like you physically *can't*? Did a doctor tell you that?"

"It doesn't take a rocket scientist—or even a doctor—to figure out that if it was possible, I'd have had at least one by now."

"Not if the guy you're with doesn't know a clitoris from his asshole."

She scrunched her nose. "Graphic much?"

"Sorry. But you know I'm right. A wise man once said, 'A clueless lover does not an orgasm make.'"

"What wise man was that?" she asked skeptically.

He smiled. "You're looking at him."

Trish rolled her eyes and lightly smacked his chest. "Listen, it's not a big deal to me. It's not like I know what I'm missing, and sex still feels good without the Big O. I only wanted you to know so you didn't pull a muscle trying or go all caveman and question your ability to make fire and kill prey with a single swing of your club." She smirked when he chuckled. "No pun intended."

"I'm not worried about my club. It's in perfect working order. But back to you," he said, still smiling, "you'd know what the big deal is if you'd gotten yourself one of those vibrating clubs. I hear they're all the rage."

"I did." He raised a questioning eyebrow. She shook her head. "Nada."

Tony sobered. "Jesus. I thought those things were foolproof."

"They probably are so long as they're not being used on a broken vagina." Doing her best to keep a grin off her face, Trish held her hands over her heart and asked, "Anthony Joseph, will you accept me as your temporary sexual partner despite my broken vagina? Speak now, or forever hold your penis."

"Wow, decisions, decisions." He pretended to waffle on an answer like a contestant on the *Price Is Right*. She gave him her best *I'm not amused* look—even though she totally was—prompting him to act.

Sinking his left hand between her thighs, he hooked her left leg and used it to pull her across the leather bench until she was tucked against him. He completely dominated the space with his wide chest and shoulders and his height advantage that forced her to tip her head back to meet his eyes. Eyes that no longer sparked with humor, but burned with the embers of carnal possibilities.

"If it's all the same to you, I'd like to go ahead with the sex portion of our evening," he said, his now-husky voice creating goose bumps all over her body. "But with one small caveat."

"What caveat is that?" Trish barely recognized the breathy voice as her own. Her body flinched like she'd touched an electric fence when his hand slid up her inner thigh until most of it disappeared under her jean skirt.

"I want you to say that you *can* in fact have an orgasm. That your body is more than capable of experiencing the ultimate release."

"I know what you're trying to do, but positive affirmations aren't—"

Tony's words came out in a quiet, but sharp command. "Stop talking unless you plan on repeating what I just told you."

Her eyes opened wide. Whoa. The amiable school teacher had left the building, and in his place was a man who knew what he wanted and expected to get it. *Holyshitthatwashot.* Her pulse started to race, and the butterflies she'd thought long dead danced in her stomach. It felt so damn good. Like, she-didn't-remember-it-ever-being-like-this damn good. And she wanted more.

Then, as if he'd read her mind, his fingers—the ones mere inches from her sex—began tracing feather-light designs along her sensitive skin. She held her breath when they got close to the damp silk covering her, but retreated at the last second, causing her to whimper her disappointment.

The sound seemed to test Tony's patience. With a disapproving sound of his own, he dipped his head and nuzzled along her jawline and the shell of her ear. "You're thinking too hard, Trish. Say it. Tell me what I want and what I know you need to hear."

Swallowing hard, she let her eyes drift closed to give her the sense of hiding even as she made herself vulnerable. "I can h-have an orgasm."

He nipped her earlobe. She gasped. "And?"

"And my body is more than capable of experiencing the ultimate release." *If only it were true.*

"Good girl." Pulling back slightly, he held her gaze with a soft intensity. Strong enough to prevent her from escaping, yet gentle enough not to harm her. Like one would hold a dove before releasing it to the sky. He made her feel cherished and protected with nothing more than a look. "I know you don't believe it now, but you will."

"What makes you so sure?"

"I figured out the problem, and I know how to fix it."

God, she'd never cared before, but suddenly Trish could think of nothing she wanted more. Not for her, but for him. "What do you think it is?" she whispered.

"That's for me to know..." His hands came up to frame her face as his lips ghosted over hers when he said the last half of something they used to say all the time growing up. "And for you to find out."

Then he kissed her deep and long, as though staking his claim, and in the back of her mind, she couldn't help but wonder if it was on her body, her potential orgasms...or something more.

～

SCENTS OF JASMINE and fresh-cut grass hung heavy in the warm air. Though it was June, the night had cooled off enough to keep the windows up while driving. But with the heat their bodies were throwing off now, the cab of the truck would be a sauna in no time.

Kissing Trish was ten times sexier than anything he'd ever done with other women. It felt different. Not physically, but the intentions behind it. Her kiss wasn't edged with ulterior motives or her own agenda. She'd opened herself up, laid herself bare, and invited him in. And nothing could have stopped him from walking through that door. Not a damn thing.

He slid his left hand down to the side of her neck until his fingertips rested along her jaw. Gentle pressure guided her to tilt her head to him, giving him deeper access. As he licked into her hot mouth and swirled around her soft tongue, it made him think of what it'd be like when he tasted and explored her wet pussy in the same way.

Anticipation and the spicy scent of her arousal tightened the noose around his balls, urging him to go faster. His body demanded he ruck up her skirt, hook her panties to the side, and sink as far as he could go inside her slick heat. If she were someone else, that's exactly what he'd do. But he didn't want to take her so casually their first time. Besides, tonight he had a mission to prove she wasn't broken, and he intended to see it through.

Things changed for him when Trish opened up about her previous sex life. He no longer thought she was merely suffering from a bad breakup. People went through those all the time; it was a part of life, like a rite of passage. He'd gone through one himself when his fiancée called off their engagement and moved across the country on a whim three years ago.

But, if Tony's instincts were right, not only did that piece of shit break her heart, he broke her spirit and her confidence, too.

He'd known guys like Nick before. They tended to belittle their wives or girlfriends. Convincing them using subtle manipulation that the women needed the men and were lucky to have them. Fucking disgraceful.

So instead of riding the wave of thoughts of all the torrid and wild things they would do together, he shoved all of that aside to take a different approach. One that should have been done with her forever ago. He was going to show her how it feels to be wanted. To be worshipped by a man's mouth, his hands, and yes, even his cock.

More importantly, he was going to make her come. Or die trying.

Tony trailed wet kisses down her neck and moved his hand over her collar bone to settle on her right breast. Her nipple met his thumb in a tight bud straining against the material. He wanted to keep going, but his neck was starting to cramp from turning it to the side. Now that she'd loosened up again and let the mood strip her inhibitions, he'd take her in the house and do things properly. But he couldn't stand the thought of being separated from her, even for the short distance across his yard to get to his front door.

"Come here, baby." The order wasn't needed since he took her by the hips and moved her to straddle his lap. She'd be able to lock her legs around his waist as they got out of the truck, and he'd have his hands on her sweet ass all the way to the house.

But Trish had other ideas. Before he even had the chance pull on the door handle, she lowered herself onto his jeans-encased cock and began rubbing on him in tiny circles.

"*Fuck,*" he hissed, throwing his head back and grinding his molars into dust.

She froze. "Oh my God, did I hurt you? Shit, I'm so sorry, Tony."

Jesus, she thought she *hurt* him? He didn't even know what to think about that. She hadn't had her V-card in a long-ass time, but mentally she was as clueless as a virgin. What kind of a prickless dick—yeah, it was an oxymoron, but whatever, it fit—was her ex that she didn't even have experience grinding on a man's erection?

Lightly pressing a finger over her lips, he shushed her until she stopped apologizing. Then he held the sides of her face and made sure she saw the truth in his eyes. "You didn't hurt me."

"I didn't?" she asked in a small voice.

He shook his head before dipping down to lick the spot below her ear. "Not even close." He kept his lips barely touching her skin and his voice low and slow to let the vibrations light up her nerve endings. "There's nothing you'll do that'll hurt me. Follow your body's instincts. It knows what it wants, even if you don't."

Her hands fisted the front of his T-shirt as her head lolled back on her shoulders. "How will I know when it wants something wrong? Or something you won't like?"

Tony mentally laughed at the idea of not liking something about sex. Impossible, especially if it was with her. He stopped kissing her neck and brought her head forward again to look him in the eyes. He gave her a reassuring grin as he brushed a curl off her flushed cheek. "There's nothing I don't like, sweetheart, believe me. And if I start swearing like a sailor, it's only because you're killing me."

"But in a good way," she clarified.

"A very, *very* good way." His gaze dropped to her mouth where he thumbed her kissed-swollen lower lip. *Damn, that's sexy.*

That would've been the perfect time to take her out of the humid truck and into the house where he could lay her out and do things the right way. Unfortunately, most of the blood in his brain had flowed south for wilder pastures in his pants, and the logic and common sense areas were always the first to get drained. So when she tugged his T-shirt up his chest, it was no surprise the only thing he thought to do was help her take it off. She rewarded his cooperation with hands that roamed over the ridges of his tanned muscles, and he hissed in a breath when her nails lightly scraped over his flat nipples.

Trish lifted her eyes to meet his. He was surprised to see hints of wonder and amusement. "Would you be insulted if I said that you're beautiful?"

A wry smile spread over his face. He'd never been so glad that he stayed faithful to his grueling workouts as he was right then. "Not at all," he said. "But I draw the line at cute or adorable."

She pretended to think about it while unsuccessfully keeping a straight face then nodded. "I'll take your request under consideration, but I make no promises."

Tony raised an eyebrow and grunted in response. Her short laugh caused her full breasts to brush his chest and that was the end of any thoughts of retaliation. The caveman switch had been thrown, cutting everything down to a single-minded desire—no, *need*—to see, touch, and taste.

He lowered his chin to home in on his targets, the anticipation nearly choking him to finally see them bared. His hot gaze
flicked up to hers from beneath his lashes and dropped the tone
of his voice to set her on edge. "Now it's my turn to play."

She swallowed hard, but otherwise hid her anxiety well. *Challenge accepted, sweetheart.* Letting his knuckles graze her soft skin,
he grabbed the hem of her tank and slowly lifted it up her flat
stomach, her ribs, and stayed bunched above her breasts. He'd be
able to pull it down quick if anyone came by.

At last he allowed himself to look...his Neanderthal faltered,
causing his inner monologue to leak a raspy *"Fuck me"* through
his lips.

Sheer white cups trimmed in lace easily displayed the dusky
color of her nipples, making his mouth water and his dick a steel
rod. It was exactly the sort of bra he'd pictured her in hundreds of
times over the years. But even his vivid imagination hadn't
conjured up the perfection of reality.

She was an angel, both inside and out. For any man to treat
her as less or let her think otherwise for even a second was a sin.
He wanted to pamper her, shower her with affection, and make
every day her happiest. But going to those extremes under the
terms of their current situation would overwhelm her and push
her away. The thought of her changing her mind about whatever
this was grated on him in the very marrow of his bones.

If the mental stuff was too much, he'd channel it all into the
physical. He'd make her come every time, multiple times. Muscle
memory would set in, and whenever she got aroused in the
future, her body would want *him.*

The temperature had jacked up to sweltering in the cab, and
a light sheen of condensation pooled on her skin. Or maybe his
mind was conjuring the erotic image out of a need to trace his
name on her chest with his tongue. He *would* mark her as his,
in time. With restrained urgency, he rubbed her nipples with
his fingers, lightly at first, causing a heavy exhale to shudder

from her lips. Then, he experimented with more pressure and even a pinch. He paid attention to her responses, her body language, and learned what she liked and what drove her fucking insane. He wanted her on level with him, and he'd lost every shred of his sanity the minute she'd started dry humping his cock.

Needing more of her, he bent to lick and tease a nipple through the thin fabric of her bra until his wetness soaked through. Unable to torture either of them any longer, he pushed the cups up to join her shirt, then drew as much of her succulent flesh into his mouth as he could. He ate at her, sucked hard, and flicked the tip of his tongue over the hard nub.

Her back arched until her shoulder blades hit the top of the steering wheel. Fingers tangled in his hair and fisted in frustration. The sting at his scalp shot down his back and wrapped his spine in a pleasure pain he craved. Hinting at his intentions, he gave her a rough scrape up her puckered areola with the edge of his lower teeth. When she moaned and spread her thighs farther apart so she could rest more firmly on his cock, he nipped the hard bud, turning the moan into a sharp intake of breath and ended with a soft whimper as he licked it all better.

"The sounds you make are incredible." He pivoted his hips to punctuate his words and to stimulate her everywhere at once. "Every moan. Every hitch of your breath. It's like you're fucking my mind. I could come just from listening to you."

"Oh my God," she breathed. "That's so hot."

Laving his tongue over the swells of her breasts, he repeated everything on the other side. She was rocking her sex across his now, even more responsive than the first time, and she scratched lines across his upper back and whispered unintelligible prayers with his name mixed in.

She was making him crazy. He'd been around the block plenty of times, and yet ten minutes with this woman had already taken him so far beyond anything he'd had with other lovers. It shouldn't be possible. Hell, it shouldn't even be *probable*. And yet he couldn't deny it even if he wanted to.

"Tony, please, I need more." He felt her hand slip between them before she cupped his balls over his jeans and squeezed. "More of *you*."

A half-groan, half-growl escaped from his chest. "You keep that up and I won't have the restraint needed to get us into the house."

"Then let's not go in."

"It's an oven in here, T. You'll suffocate."

"I don't care." Trish grabbed the sides of his face and pinned him with hungry eyes. "This feels too good. I don't want to lose this feeling. I can't, not yet."

He heard what she wasn't saying. She was afraid if they changed anything, whatever the reason her body was finally reacting as strongly as it should wouldn't still work. He wasn't about to get into that with her; she'd realize it on her own when sex felt better each time they came together and he learned her body and what it liked.

For now, he was more than happy taking her right where they sat. Tony reached behind her to twist the ignition a click and lower the windows several inches. They both sighed as a breeze bent and flowed around their bodies, cooling their heated skin.

"Better?" he asked as he nipped and kissed a path up her offered neck.

"Mmmm, much, thank you."

"Welcome." He cut his reply short, not wanting to waste the extra beat it would take to say the additional syllable before he claimed her mouth with a searing kiss. Her arms wrapped around his neck and pulled them together so her breasts mashed to his chest. Losing themselves in the moment again, any sensations that had slowed to a simmer from their brief pause were again climbing to mercurial levels.

"Anthony Joseph," she snapped out between harsh breaths, "if you don't get your pants off in the next ten seconds, I'm climbing out of this truck and walking my happy ass home."

With that, he had the front of his jeans undone and shoved halfway down his ass along with his boxer briefs, freeing his erection. She smiled her satisfaction against his lips and whispered, "Took you long enough," before sliding her hand down the ridges of his abdomen. Her destination was obvious and his body coiled tight with anticipation and the effort it took to hold himself back.

Fingertips smoothed the slippery liquid seeping from the tip around his hyper-sensitive cock head. "Oh, fuck," he said on a grunt. "Yeah, baby, keep touching me."

She hummed against his neck and trailed her hand over his full length before sitting back and peering down. He followed her gaze, barely noting how his stiff cock rested along the line of his abs and over his navel. What drew his attention was the stark difference between their states of undress. While he was naked down to his thighs, she still wore panties, a bunched up skirt and her bra and tank shoved above her chest. Tony scowled, trying to make her clothes spontaneously combust, but no such luck.

"You're um..." She cleared her throat. "You're bigger than what I'm used to."

He held her face and forced her to look at him, ready to thank her for the compliment until he saw the very real concern in her eyes. His brows drew together. "By how much?"

She swallowed hard. "*Very* much."

Tony reminded himself that now was not the time to mentally gloat about dwarfing her ex's dick, but he still felt his chest puff up, even if only metaphorically. He needed to focus on reassuring Trish or he wouldn't have anything to be proud about.

"I know it doesn't seem like it, but I promise you'll open up for me," he said softly. Reaching behind her, he used one hand to hold her panties to the side and inserted a thick finger from his right hand deep inside her. Trish sucked in a breath and bucked against his hand. "I'll show you."

For several minutes he helped her hot channel stretch around his fingers until he had his three longest ones thrusting deep inside her. "Oh my God," she moaned. His left arm banded around her waist and pulled her in tight. Her juices dripped down his hand and onto his balls and bare thighs. *More. Need more, always more.*

Using his hands, he tilted her pelvis and... "There," he grunted as he notched the head of his dick at the top of her folds to hit the right spot.

"*Uhn!*" she cried with a jolt, then she pressed her forehead to his as though needing the contact to ground herself in the moment. He couldn't deny needing the same thing as his breaths sawed in and out.

After a few experimental movements, she got the hang of how to use him to stimulate her clit. Little by little she quickened her pace and he synced his fingers with it, reveling in the way her inner walls sucked harder against his retreats.

"Fuck yes," he said through clenched teeth. "Just like that, baby. Feel good?"

She nodded. Her lax expression told him she'd left the ability for coherent speech behind. Perfect. The only language she spoke now came from her gorgeous body.

He'd planned to hold out until he'd made her come at least once with his fingers, but a man was only so strong. If he didn't get inside her right now, he'd lose his mind, not to mention his pride when he shot his load all over his stomach.

"Trish," he gritted out. "Condom. Wallet, right back pocket." She surprised him when she found it without any problems and tossed his wallet off to the side as soon as she had the prize in her hand. "Roll it on me so I can feel this wet pussy surrounding my cock. You're ready."

In seconds he was sheathed and poised at her opening. He nudged her channel and moaned an exhale in a rush. It'd contracted again, making it a snug fit despite his fingers having just left her. He let her control the speed as she lowered herself onto his shaft. Inch by excruciating fucking inch, the woman he'd wanted more than any other took him into her body.

"That's it, baby, only a little bit more." She nodded, but held still for a moment, trying to catch her breath. Or maybe from a hint of trepidation at how he filled her so completely. "Trish, we don't have to go any farther. You're in control. Right now is probably as far as my fingers could go, and I know that felt good to you, didn't it?"

Again, she nodded. "Yes," she whispered.

"Good. So if you want to start moving and make it feel good again, I'm on board." He paused, kissing her lips and teasing her with his tongue. "No matter what you do, I'm going to love it, so I'll follow your lead."

"I don't want to stop. You feel so good, Tony. I want all of you, I do. I'm just a little nervous," she said with a half-shrug.

His hand wrapped around the back of her neck and pulled her in. He loved how small she felt to him, how easily she let him command her body. Speaking into her ear, he said, "Would you like me to help you sink all the way onto my cock, Trish? Until I'm so fucking deep inside you there's no way to tell where I end and you begin?"

A quiet whimper accompanied her nod.

Fire raced through his veins. He'd never been so turned on in his life, and it was giving him ideas he never would've considered before. Being with Trish—*in* Trish—took him to a whole new level of sexual awareness, and he knew exactly how to help her.

Tony took hold of her hands and pulled them behind her, then through the bottom half of the steering wheel to place them on his knees. So fucking beautiful. The position gave her a way to brace herself and also kept her arched back so he had the perfect view of where he disappeared inside her. And how much more of him still needed in.

Drops of sweat gathered and spilled over the swells and

between her full, rounded tits begging for attention. His hands covered them, squeezed, released, then pinched the tips of her taut nipples, steadily increasing the pressure. He watched her eyes closely, waiting for them to tell him when it crossed from pleasure to pain and just beyond.

Now.

Instantly he released them to let the blood flow back into the red buds, causing her to throw her head back and cry out his name and God's several times over. A new flood of warmth bathed his cock, and he used it to slide home the last couple of inches.

He had to move or he'd die. He was sure of it. "Are you okay?" he panted. "Trish, sweetheart, talk to me."

She didn't offer him words, but something better. Her hips began grinding on his, back and forth, keeping him fully seated. "I can't believe how good this feels. When you let go, I felt like lightning shot from my nipples straight to my clit. Was that...?"

"I have no doubt it felt amazing, but no. You didn't come." Her bottom lip stuck out with her eyebrows drawn in. How in the hell did she make a pout look sexy?

"How do you know?"

"Keep holding on to my legs like you are, and let me do all the work."

Bracing his feet on the floorboard, Tony thrust his hips up deep and hard, over and over. His hands splayed over the crease where thigh met body and his thumbs met in the middle over her clit. One pulled the skin above it tight to expose the swollen bundle of nerves while the other teased it mercilessly.

Tony studied every detail about her. He wanted the image of her in this moment to be burned into his mind. The way her damp skin glowed in the moonlight. How wisps of her loose curls stuck to her face and neck. How sexy she looked with her shirt shoved up, her nipples hard and red from his attention. Parted, swollen lips and hooded eyes glazed over with lust.

"Oh God, it feels...I don't know..." She whimpered and shook her head. "Tony, I-- *Shit*, it's too much."

She freed her arms out and plowed her hands into his hair, fisting large chunks and pulling in frustration. He didn't slow, didn't relent. "You're almost there, keep going."

Squeezing her eyes shut tight, she shook her head again. "I don't think I can take it."

"Yes, you can," he said. "Open your eyes and look at me. Trish, *look* at me."

Finally, she listened. Endless dark pools stared back at him, searching for an answer on how to deal with the overwhelming sensations flooding her. "Just hold on to me and let me take you over that edge. *Trust me.*"

Trish dug her teeth into her bottom lip and nodded, curling her body over him to rest her forehead on his shoulder as he continued to pleasure her.

She had no idea how much she humbled him. She trusted him to bring her pleasure she couldn't foresee and didn't believe was possible for her. Knowing that alone would have brought him to his knees had he been standing. He didn't take her offering lightly or for granted, and he would do everything possible to make this experience one that she'd never forget.

Gritting his teeth through the strain of beating back the fire swirling in his balls, he drove her closer to what had been denied her for too damn long. "You're so perfect," he rasped against her ear. "I love your pussy. So hot and tight and wet. I want to feel you come, baby. Feel you tighten on me like a fucking vise."

Finally, he felt her body start its climb to oblivion. Knowing she was about to topple from riding the knife's edge made him double his efforts. "Oh God oh shit *oh God oh shit*—"

Tony clamped a hand over her mouth just before she screamed into the stillness of the night. Her nails bit into the skin on his shoulders as she convulsed around his cock so hard he swore his vision blacked out. Moments later he groaned long and loud as she milked his balls of his own release for what seemed like an eternity.

Time had no meaning in the aftermath. They clung to each other, a tangle of sweaty limbs and twisted clothes, panting like dogs lazing in the sun. It might have been only a few minutes or it might have been close to an hour, Tony didn't know. What he did know, was that he wasn't the same man he'd been before sex with Trish Howell. His life would forever be split into two time periods: before sex with Trish and after sex with Trish. It didn't lend itself to catchy acronyms, but he couldn't ignore that a line had been drawn.

She had raised the bar and now his standards for what he considered "good sex" might be unreachable by any other woman. Figured there'd be a catch to finally getting the one girl he'd wanted longer than he could remember wanting anything else. He'd just have to make sure he got as much of her as he could so he had an entire library of memories to call on after she left town.

Kissing her temple, he began straightening her clothes. "What are you thinking, T?"

Flushed and beautiful, she smiled the smile of a woman well-sexed. "I'm thinking that you fixed me."

"You were never broken." Tony lifted a hand and rubbed the side of his thumb over her cheekbone. "You just didn't have a man who knew how to make your body sing."

"Then I'm glad I have one now," she admitted softly. Then quickly added, "Even if it's only for a little while."

He managed a half-smile and hoped she assumed he was too exhausted to put more effort into it. As much as it bothered him to think of her leaving again, the reminder was for the best. He had to keep a level perspective of what this was, and what it wasn't. Otherwise his heart might not survive the summer.

"In that case," he quipped, "think of me as your temporary

voice coach. I'll be happy to give you lessons as often as you want, all for the low, low price of feeding my ego."

"Hmm. What if I want the *American Idol* package?" At his raised brow, she explained. "I'd like enough lessons that I could audition for *AI* if I wanted. You know, teach me all the advanced singing stuff. How much would that cost?"

Lots of sex with advanced moves thrown in? Hellfuckingyes! He'd probably pay *her* for that plan if she demanded it. He didn't have *that* much pride. But he had a better idea. "I can teach you the advanced stuff no problem. But the cost will be your trust. You'll have to trust me that I'll only ever do anything to bring you pleasure. You do that, and you'll be able sing whatever you want. Deal?"

Her smile shined in the moonlight and she gave him a sharp nod. "Deal."

CHAPTER FIVE

Trish made her way over to the large soccer field where Tony had told her his youth team, the Shark Bytes, was playing. The game had started a half hour ago, but she'd had to work and told him she'd be over after her shift. Parents and siblings filled the bleachers along one side of the field watching the wee munchkins in blue jerseys mixing with the other team's green ones.

She found an open spot on the bottom riser and settled in. Tony was striding along the sideline, keeping in step with the action of the game. He looked great in his matching blue jersey and black athletic shorts, and she smiled as he cupped his hands around his mouth to yell instructions to his players in what seemed like a futile attempt at directing chickens with their heads cut off.

He hadn't yet seen her, which was fine with her. She didn't want to distract him, plus she enjoyed having this time to study him in his element without him knowing. The last few weeks with Tony had been...well, pretty amazing. She'd been worried that adding sex to their longtime friendship would make things awkward or complicated, but it was exactly the opposite.

It felt like a natural progression for their relationship. They'd always cared a great deal for each other and had fun together. It was easy for Trish to be around Tony. He never pressured her to talk about her past or her future like Rhianna and her mom, and he certainly never felt the need to define their current situation or ask if it was going anywhere. With him, she felt relaxed and carefree. So it was no small wonder why she didn't mind spending the majority of her free time with him.

He'd suggested keeping things exclusive-casual—which she agreed to—and he even went so far as to pretend she wasn't crazy when she made beds a no-no. To Trish, two people could screw on a couch and even fall asleep with each other afterward and not feel like an invisible line has been crossed. But that same scenario in a bed changed the whole dynamic. And as far as she was concerned, their "dynamic" was fine the way it was. And by *fine* she meant panty-scorching, mind-blowing amazing.

That first time in the truck had demolished all her past assumptions that she somehow was incapable of enjoying sex, much less experiencing an orgasm. Tony made her burn hotter than she ever thought possible, and he didn't even need his body to do it. His words alone could likely make her come. The brain was a powerful thing, and the things he said to her—whether sweet and flattering or salacious and filthy—made her just as wet, if not more, as when he touched her.

Therefore, after reviewing all of the evidence presented to this court, Trish's ex was found guilty of being a pathetic lover in the first degree. *Goodbye and good riddance.*

The shrill sound of a whistle blowing brought her out of her relationship musings and back to the present entertainment. Over the course of the next thirty minutes, she laughed at the antics of both teams. It wasn't exactly a structured game with plays and positions, but rather every player from both teams chasing the ball. It looked like the ball was a powerful magnet

and the players were metal shavings that were helpless to be
pulled along after it.

During a time out, Tony had glanced over at the bleachers
and finally noticed her. She gave him a small finger wave and he
returned it with a brilliant smile and wink. A little blonde girl
had seen the interaction and immediately announced to the rest
of the team in the huddle that "Mr. Tony just winked at that
pretty girl," which instigated a roar of dramatic oohs and giggles
and even a few boys singing the "k-i-s-s-i-n-g" song.

Trish felt her cheeks grow hot as dozens of eyes drilled her
from the crowd and snickers of laughter drifted on the slight
breeze. Tony brought them back under control like a professional
cat wrangler and sent them back onto the field. As soon as he
made sure the correct amount of players were in the game with
the rest of the team safely behind the boundary line, he looked
over his shoulder at her and mouthed "sorry." She smiled and
waved it off.

For the rest of the game, she rarely turned her gaze to the
action on the field, preferring to study Tony and how he inter-
acted with the kids. He was amazing with them. Clapping and
cheering any time one of them made an attempt to kick the ball
into the goal or even if they unsuccessfully tried to kick it away
from an opposing player. He got the kids who weren't currently
playing excited to cheer for their teammates and changed players
often so everyone got fair amounts of play time. And when he
crouched down to comfort a boy who'd cried after the ball hit
him in the face, her heart squeezed inside her chest. A couple
minutes later, the boy nodded at his coach and wiped his tears
away before smiling and running back out to play.

When the whistle blew and the Shark Bytes won 2-0, Tony's
team erupted into screams and cheers and bounced around like
the grass was made of trampolines. He directed them to line up
and slap the other team's hands, following after them to do the
same thing and then shake the hand of the other coach. One of

the parents opened up a cooler full of juice boxes and another held out a container of orange wedges. The kids swarmed both and got their post-game snacks. While they were busy with that, Trish approached Tony from behind.

"Congratulations, Coach," she said.

Turning around, his face lit up and he instantly pulled her into his arms. "Hey there, sexy. I'm glad you came. I thought maybe you'd changed your mind after working all day."

"Well, I did have visions of a hot bath and foot soak dancing in my head, but I couldn't pass up the chance to finally see the deadly Shark Bytes in action. I definitely made the right choice, because that was thoroughly entertaining," she said. "The drama on the field is more intense than an episode of the *Kardashians*. I loved every minute of it. Two enthusiastic thumbs up."

He laughed and they looked at the kids running around and shoving the oranges in their mouths so the rinds took the place of their teeth in their big smiles. "Yeah, they're pretty great. I enjoy teaching, but I love coaching these guys. Hands down my favorite job."

"They're lucky to have such an amazing, not to mention incredibly handsome, coach. You're really good with them, babe."

Leaning close, he spoke low against her ear. "I know someone else I'd like to be really good with." Her breath caught in her chest, and he answered with a quiet growl. "Scratch that. I wanna be really bad with her. And I want her to be dirty as hell with me."

She clutched at his shirt between them and prayed her weak knees didn't give out as vibrations of desire rolled through her belly. "I'm willing to bet she'd be more than okay with that," she said on an exhale.

"Oh, I have no doubt," he said. "Unfortunately, she'll have to wait a couple hours until after I play in my game."

"What? That's not fair. You brought it up, now you have to deliver."

"Wish I could." His wicked half-grin showed none of the remorse his words implied. "But the game starts in less than thirty minutes across town, so we have to leave as soon as I get these rascals sent off." Tony played in an adult soccer league. He didn't make all the practices—because he was coaching the Shark Bytes and sometimes because he was giving her mind-blowing orgasms—but he made them when he could and most of the games.

"You're a cruel man, Anthony Joseph. If I wasn't so fond of you —and my orgasms—I'd make you suffer through your game tonight with a massive erection."

He scoffed. "Like I don't already walk around half hard when-ever you're with me. But the good news is, the game is at the fields a block from my place, so after I kick Jefferson's ass, I can have you naked and on my couch in under two minutes flat."

"Mmm, now you're speaking my language."

He chuckled. "I thought I might be. Wait here, then we can go."

Trish nodded and he gave her a quick kiss before calling his team together for a post-game huddle. After congratulating them on their awesome hustling and team spirit, Tony reminded them of their game the following week and led them in a team cheer. As soon as it was over, the kids scattered in all directions to meet up with their parents waiting for them.

Tony grabbed a mesh bag full of practice soccer balls and made his way back to her. When they reached his car, he tossed the bag in the back seat. The tech class had their final earlier that week, so Trish opened the passenger side door that was almost good as new after the tech ed class replaced it for their final and sat inside. As soon as she clicked her seatbelt in, he was right there, leaning over to capture her face in his hands and claim her mouth with a wild urgency.

She opened for him on a whimper of answering need and met his lashing tongue with her own. He angled her head and took the kiss deeper. Her hands gripped his muscular forearms in a desperate attempt to ground herself to the man currently stealing her breath and making her forget everything but him.

When he broke their connection to rest his forehead on hers, the only sounds were of their labored breaths and her heart beating rapidly against her ribcage.

"You have no idea how badly I want to touch you and get you off right now," he rasped.

"I think I have a pretty good idea. I was thinking the same thing about you."

Releasing a groan of frustration, he nipped at her bottom lip. "As soon as the game ends, you're mine."

"You mean when we get back to your place."

"You'll be lucky if I wait that long." Tony reached down and cupped her sex over her jean shorts, aka Daisy Dukes. She hadn't been able to resist. "I know you didn't wear these to work, which means you deliberately changed after, knowing I'd be out of my fucking mind as soon as I saw you in them. Am I right?"

Perhaps shedding her city apparel for a more casual look was something she should do permanently. Trish willed herself not to blush as she tried for a look of innocence. "I'm sure I don't know what you mean, Tony. It's hot out tonight so I opted for shorts just like everyone else."

"You're such a bad liar, T." A wicked grin tugged one corner of his mouth up. "I'll say it again. As soon as the game ends, *this*," he said, squeezing his hand possessively, "is mine. You can think about that while you're watching me play, and know that every time I look over at you, I'm imagining you naked and writhing beneath me."

An involuntary squeak in the back of her throat preceded her whisper. "Shit."

~

TRISH HAD NEVER THOUGHT MUCH about the sport of soccer one way or the other. She knew David Beckam was a soccer player, and she'd gladly watch that man do anything, but she never considered that he might not be the only man to look hot while kicking a spotted ball.

Turned out, she thought a lot of the guys who played in tonight's game were hot. Not necessarily because of what they looked like, but because of how they moved on the field. Quick, agile, with unbelievable control over the ball using their entire bodies except their hands.

She loved watching the game, despite that it started to sprinkle somewhere around halfway through. The air was warm so it didn't bother her enough to seek shelter or spring an umbrella like the few people did who stayed to stick it out till the end of the game. Not that she had an umbrella to spring, but she wouldn't have used it even if she did. The cool raindrops felt good on her heated skin, plus it masked the signs of her wetness between her legs that had nothing to do with the damn weather.

Tony was making good on his promise to keep her aware of his intentions for her after the game. Whenever the action stopped—a timeout, the ball crossing out of bounds, a ref blew his whistle, or a goal was scored—his gaze immediately sought her out on the sidelines, holding her down as effectively as his body stretched over hers, as he stalked across the muddy grass. During one of those moments, he'd actually reached down with one large hand to palm his cock and balls, then he dragged his bottom lip from his teeth as he adjusted himself before joining the rest of his team in the huddle. The whole thing had happened in a couple of seconds, but felt like a scene played in super slo-mo. Trish thought she'd die of embarrassment, but no one seemed to catch his lascivious stunt but her. Probably because she was the only one watching him like a horny hawk. Once she realized that, she breathed a little easier and let herself enjoy the things he made her feel.

Holy shit. She didn't think it was possible for him to look any hotter than normal—how had she never noticed he had this much sex appeal before?—but right now he was like one big wet dream. Water dripped from the ends of his hair and gathered his dark lashes into spikes around those fiery golden brown eyes. The hollows of his cheeks appeared sharper, the dusting of stubble across his face more prominent. The man was wholly animalistic and the expression on his face when he stared at her promised carnal pleasures hot enough to singe the panties right off her body.

By the time the game ended, the men were covered in mud and completely soaked. They celebrated their win in the same manner as Tony's five-year olds. Bouncing around, yelling, and jumping on top of each other, until at last they lined up to "good game" the other team.

Trish waited by the bleachers for Tony, antsy and more sexed up than an ex-con in a whorehouse. Okay, that was proof she was on the brink of "crazy" because she had *no* idea where an analogy like that could have come from. On the other hand, it was a damn good analogy for how she felt. Tony could probably blow on her clit and she'd shatter.

Then she saw him reach back between his shoulder blades with one hand and yank his jersey off and all thoughts skidded to a halt. Tan muscles gleaming with sweat shifted and contracted with every move, every breath. Mud streaked across his shins and the cut planes of his calves, whereas his arms, neck, and face sported splatters from it getting kicked up when they ran.

Sweet Baby Jesus, I'm a fucking goner. Tony was finishing up with his teammates, smiles, laughter, and friendly punches all around from the men as the group slowly broke up. Trish stood on the sidewalk, waiting anxiously to see his face so she could gauge what happened next. Crossing her arms across her stomach, she wished she'd found shelter from the rain after all. She probably looked like a drowned rat. Her shorts and baby tee were soaked through and her long hair hung in stringy chunks around her face.

Then all thoughts of her appearance or anything else dissolved as Tony turned and strode toward her, blue shirt tossed over his large shoulder and cleats dangling from the fingers of one hand, with that same look he'd pinned on her all night. Suddenly she wasn't so sure of her ability to handle him in his worked up state. Glancing over her shoulder in the direction of his house, Trish took note that no one milled around behind her to witness her imminent sexual demise at the hands of Anthony DiAngelo.

"You thinking of making a run for it, gorgeous?"

Her head spun back to him, strands of her hair whipping her face. Now that he mentioned it, she definitely had a fight-or-flight thing going on. "That depends," she said, lifting her chin in a haughty gesture of absent confidence. "Do you plan on behaving like a civil human being and wait until we're behind closed doors before you attack me?"

"Attack you?" He laughed, his abs tightening and rippling, and then her knees almost buckled when he stopped several feet away and repeated his earlier practice of grabbing himself. Except this time he smoothed the shiny black athletic shorts over his impressive length that angled up and to the right, unable to point due north without exposing several inches above his elastic waistband. "Look what thinking of you does to me. You have no idea how difficult it is to run and move like I did for hours with a fucking billy club in my shorts."

Trish barked out a laugh at his description, but clapped a hand over her mouth when he dipped his head and leered at her with a deliciously evil grin. Heat vibrated deep in her center and she felt more warmth coat her panties. She thought she'd have run out of moisture by now, but it was obvious her body would always welcome him, and she had no problem with that whatsoever.

"Glad you're having a good time, T, because I'm sure as hell about to." He pulled his shirt down and wrapped his cleats in it, then secured the bundle under one arm like a football. "Hell, yes, I'm going to attack you. And then I'm going to *devour* you. I'll give you a five second head start."

"You're not serious."

"Four...three..."

Trish yelped, snatched her flip flops off, and took off at a dead run in the opposite direction toward his house, unable to stop the laughter spilling out from her even as she heard him call out "one" to signal the start of his pursuit.

The sun had set about an hour earlier and the only light illuminating the puddles and squares of concrete under her bare feet were the house lights on people's front porches. Her arms pumped hard with a sandal in each hand, and her eyes flicked between her final destination and the sidewalk in front of her so she wouldn't trip on a buckled section or step on a kid's toy left behind from the day's activities.

He was gaining on her. She heard him splash through a puddle she'd displaced only two seconds earlier. *Almost there!* Finally, she reached his driveway and cut a sharp right around his parked car on her way to his unlocked back door. But just as she started tossing mental confetti and handing herself a great big trophy, a deep chuckle slid into her ear and muscled arms banded around her waist. She squealed as he lifted her easily and swung her around to push her back against the side of the house, pinning her with his massive body.

There was no gloating, no preamble. Tony's hands held her head steady as he did as promised and quite thoroughly attacked her.

She opened to him instantly and wrapped her arms around him to hold him down by the backs of his shoulders. Or maybe it was to help lift herself up to align their bodies just right. She'd gladly climb him like a tree if it meant fitting his cock where she needed it.

"Shit, I've never been so hard and ready to fuck in my life," he growled as she licked the words from his mouth. With a firm yank, Tony pulled the fly of her shorts apart and buried his hand in the front, plunging his fingers up to the knuckles in one smooth motion. "Jesus, baby, your pussy's so wet you took all three fingers on the first try."

Trish couldn't respond. Words failed her. Thoughts failed her. He'd reduced her to a quivering mass of nerves as he stroked, sucked, and fucked, letting her float in the space where nothing existed but her pleasure. She didn't have much experience to compare him to, but she knew instinctively that Tony was an amazing lover. He did things to her, giving her whole-body orgasms that rode the sharp line between needing him to stop and threatening his life if he ever fucking stopped.

"Please," she begged as he moved his fingers in and out, "I n-need you."

He took her hand and shoved it in the waistband of his shorts. "Stroke me while I fuck you with my fingers. Get me ready to take you so hard you'll feel me deep inside you for a week."

Wrapping around his sizeable girth, she pumped up and down as best she could while he drove her insane with those magical fingers of his. When he cursed and followed it up with a sigh, Trish opened her eyes to find him definitely unhappy.

"What's wrong?"

"Condoms are inside. I wanted you right here, but looks like I'll have to plan our public trysts a little more next time."

The thought of doing things while hiding in plain sight gave her delicious shivers that rode her spine down to her sex. "Okay, let's go in then."

"I'm going to make you come first. Then we'll get nice and dirty in the shower together."

"You mean clean," she said on a gasp as he changed his position to hit her G-spot with the tips of two fingers.

He nipped her earlobe and rasped, "No I don't," then started moving his entire hand up and down as fast as he could, keeping his middle two fingers tucked inside. She felt herself get impossibly wet and heard her inner walls sucking on his thick digits in the stillness of the night.

In seconds, her body raced toward orgasm like a runaway train at top speed. "OhGodohGodohGod, yeah, right there *right there*..." Her breaths were so short and fast that her vision grew hazy on the edges, and the only sounds she could hear were those of her simpering pants she was helpless to quiet.

Tony had to know she was getting close. Her body spoke to him as clearly as if English was its native tongue. The imaginary band deep in her belly twisted more and more, ratcheting the tension inside higher and higher.

"Fuck, you're squeezing me tight." His voice was strained like he had to hold himself back from his own release just from watching her take hers. It didn't matter that he controlled the sex most of the time, because she'd learned early on that *she* had the power to bring this big man to his knees without even trying. And that was a heady feeling.

He clapped his free hand over her mouth to muffle her cries as she teetered on the razor's edge. She'd been rambling a string of *oh-fuck-oh-shit* seconds before, but speech and breathing were no longer possible as her chest clamped down on her lungs and her body bowed hard against him.

"That's it, baby, let it go," he said, his staccato pants of breath hitting her ear. "Come for me."

At last, the twisting band snapped, releasing the air in her lungs and the scream in her throat. She bucked against the hand that held her pelvis and screamed against the palm that covered her mouth as white-hot pricks of sensation rippled through her from the tips of her toes to the roots of her hair.

Her pussy clamped down so hard that it pushed his fingers from her channel with a warm rush of fluid that ran down her legs with the water still dripping from her soaked clothes. "Fuck, that's hot," Tony whispered as he dragged out her orgasm with the flat of his hand, rubbing fast and light over her swollen lips. "Yeah, keep going. Good girl."

When he finally stilled his movements to cup her sex with his strong hand, Trish started floating back to herself as the storm of sensations calmed inside her. Her scream had died down to a keening moan, enough that he took his hand away and replaced it with his lips, kissing her slowly and thoroughly. Her entire body trembled in aftershocks and she didn't know how much longer her legs would hold her up.

She sighed in relief as he bent and swept her up in his arms to hold her tight. Her post-orgasm brain didn't remember much on how they made it into his house and then his shower, but she enjoyed his silent pampering beneath the spray of hot water sluicing over her skin like silk. He cleaned them both and took extra care shampooing and conditioning her long hair. Trish briefly thought about taking over—she knew what a pain that much hair could be—but she couldn't bring herself to lift her arms or voice the offer.

After towel drying them off, he scooped her up again and stepped into the hallway, turning left to head toward the living room and the couch that had probably seen more action than a bed in a honeymoon suite.

"Wait," she said, halting his progress. With her arms looped around his neck, she peered up at him through her lashes and took a chance at altering their dynamic. "Let's go to your room."

Dark eyebrows disappeared under the wet hair hanging over his forehead. "You want me to take you to bed?" She nodded, then shivered as his look of surprise turned heated with determination. "If I put you in my bed tonight, or any night, you're staying there until morning. I don't want any lame excuses about having to leave or waking up in the middle of the night to find you on the couch."

"It's okay, I understand. I *want* to be with you like that. We already spend the night together on the couch, Tony. I'm not running from being in your arms all night. I'm just removing the no-beds rule."

"It's about damn time," he snarled. "Hated that fucking rule." Then he pulled a one-eighty and stalked to his bedroom.

TONY HAD NEVER BEEN SO happy to take a woman to bed. He supposed there was something to be said for waiting.

When he thought they were going to end up on the couch, he'd had wild and dirty ideas running through his mind on what he wanted to do to Trish. Making her come so hard that she'd bathed his hand in her juices had him so worked up he could barely think straight.

But as soon as he laid her in the middle of his king bed, all of his kinky plans changed into one immense need: to make love to her. So that's exactly what he did.

All night, Tony touched and tasted in slow motion. He left no inch of her beautiful body unkissed. The soundtrack of their love making was a mix of sharp gasps, hitches of breath, and soft moans with intermittent begging. He wished he'd set his phone to record audio because it was the most erotic thing he'd ever heard.

After hours of exploring each other and both of them coming more times than he could count, they fell into a sweat-slicked heap with her tucked back against him and their hearts beating in time together. Something big shifted in Tony's chest, and the relief he felt was so strong, he slipped into unconsciousness with a smile on his face.

CHAPTER SIX

A five-star midnight picnic. Only Tony could come up with something so perfect as to bring both the beauty of the country and some of the finer things she'd acquired a taste for over the years together in one amazing evening.

Earlier in the day, she'd cheered like crazy for the Shark Bytes as they shut out the Crazy Carp 1-0. Then Trish invited the whole team out to Fort's favorite place for cheap ice cream, Frosty Freeze, and bought the kids—and their handsome coach and tag-a-long referee, Jason—a celebratory ice cream treat. The utter chaos that came from controlling twenty kindergarteners with sloppy faces and sticky fingers had been totally worth it to see their smiles.

As the last player left with his parents and the stern promise of a very long bath, Tony told her he had something special planned for them that night. He said to wear something Sunday casual, which meant nice enough to go to church, yet comfortable enough to enjoy the church picnic the rest of the day. She'd opted for a simple sundress and had brought a light sweater wrap to keep her arms warm if the air got chilly when the sun went down.

He'd picked her up around nine, just before dusk, and they drove out to a secluded area along Lake Koshkonong where nothing surrounded them but the sky above and the grass below. They laid out a thick blanket on the grass and watched the sunset melt into the water's horizon as they enjoyed their late meal. He'd brought several kinds of sushi for her, which she'd grown to love in New York, and some dry rub chicken wings for himself, along with an amazing fruit salad for dessert with their sparkling wine.

Trish smiled from a high dose of contentment as she sipped from a plastic flute, reveling in the tiny bubbles bursting with flavor on her tongue before sliding down her throat and warming her insides. "Mmm, this tastes so good," she said, handing him her empty glass, "but if I have any more you'll have to carry me into bed later."

Chuckling, he said, "It certainly wouldn't be the first time."

"Touché." She often fell asleep on his couch while they chilled in front of the television at night, and since the "no beds" rule had gone out the window several weeks back, he always texted Rhi to let her know Trish would be spending the night so she didn't worry, and then tucked her into bed next to him. She'd been concerned at first, but nothing had ever been the least bit awkward. On the contrary, it allowed them the opportunity to wake each other up in new and creative ways, and now she stayed at his place more often than not.

On a sigh of satisfaction, she lowered herself to her back on the picnic quilt and gazed up at the blanket of stars, wondering idly how lucky she was to have the best summer of her life when she'd thought a few short months ago that it would surely be her worst.

Tony set everything off to the side and lay next to her, his body turned in and his head rested on his hand so he could look down on her. With his free hand, he drew lazy designs on the multitude of skin left exposed by her dress, causing her to shiver.

"Are you cold?" he asked.

She smiled. "No. I wasn't shivering from being cold."

He gave her a knowing smile in return as he dropped his head to kiss her long and leisurely. "I think you taste a hell of a lot better than that champagne," he said between licks.

"Sparkling wine."

Kiss, lick. "Hmm?"

Sigh, kiss. "It's sparkling wine. It can only be called champagne if it comes from France."

He lowered his voice and made it sound dark and smooth, like audible sex. "Mmm, I love it when talk city to me, baby. Describe the smell of a taxi. In detail."

They both started laughing and then swapping ideas back and forth, trying to one-up each other on dirty city things.

"Say the word for a fried snail," he said with a dramatic groan.

"Tell me the current rat-to-person ratio in the Big Apple," she said breathily.

"Ooh, how about the closing status of the Dow Jones today?"

Trish dissolved into a fit of giggles. Perhaps the wine was more potent than she thought. "You really know how to make a girl hot, don't you, Mr. DiAngelo? Must be those Italian genes of yours."

"They don't call us Italian Stallions for nothing, Ms. Howell," he said with a smirk.

"Italian Stallion." Reaching up she trailed her hand over the side of his face, his five o'clock shadow tickling her palm. "I don't know that all Italian men deserve the moniker, but the name certainly suits you," she mused softly.

Turning his face in, he placed a kiss to the center of her palm and then the sensitive underside of her wrist. "Trish, there's a reason I brought you here tonight."

"Is it to make love to me beneath the stars?" she asked, hopeful.

The white teeth of his smile shone from the half-moon hanging low in the sky. "That's not the reason, but I'm hoping it'll be a nice side benefit."

"Me, too. What do I have to do to ensure such a wonderful benefit occurs?"

"I have some things I want to tell you. All you have to do is listen."

"Sounds easy enough. Okay, I'm listening." She gave him an approving nod as though he were a subordinate asking for permission to proceed from his superior. Another example of their effortless banter and likeminded humor that kept them in stitches more often than not.

Trish hadn't realized how lackluster her life in New York had been until she had these few months to compare it to. Not that she never laughed during her relationship with Nick or moped around in a perpetual state of gloom. But when she put her mind to it, she couldn't recall any instances where they'd flat out belly-laughed until their sides hurt or tears streaked down their faces. With Tony, it was damn near a daily occurrence.

Still lying on his side, Tony held himself up with his forearm tucked under him. His free arm snaked around her waist to pull her in and eliminate the offensive inches of space dividing them. How *dare* they. Trish almost giggled at her own joke, but stifled it when she saw the seriousness of the matter in Tony's expression.

"Hey, you know you can tell me anything, right?" she whispered.

He answered with a thoughtful nod, then brought her left hand up to place a kiss on the backs of her fingers. "When my family moved to town in third grade, I'd left behind several friends that I'd known my whole life. So you can imagine how I felt about starting a new school in a small town where everyone had been friends since pre-school or longer. I was an angry kid. I did a lot of lashing out at home and planned to do more of the same at school. I foolishly thought that if my parents realized I wouldn't get any better here, they'd move us back to our old home.

"Then I saw you on the first day of school, and everything else faded into the distance. You were so happy all the time and full of life. Everyone adored you, students and teachers alike. Part of me envied you your close friends because it reminded me of how much I missed mine. And still another part of me resented you for being so popular and loved. Most of me, though, just wanted to be near you, but you weren't paying much attention to the new kid. So I stole your softball glove."

"*That's* why you took my glove?" Trish rocked her head back and forth in astonishment and grinned up at the goofy boy. "You know you could have just asked me to play tag or something, right?"

"Yeah, well, you were like mental kryptonite. Anytime you came close, my I.Q. instantly dropped several points," he said wryly. "Illegal possession of personal property seemed like a great idea at the time."

"Hmm, and how'd that plan work out for you?" It was a rhetorical question, of course. Everyone knew his shin had gotten a swift introduction to her foot and had the bruise to show for it.

"Short-term? Not so hot. But in the long run..." His light brown eyes appeared cool and metallic in what little light the moon gave them, and yet she felt as if they burned through her, heating her from the inside out. "I'm here, lying under the stars with you on a beautiful night, and when we're done here, I'm taking you back to my bed. I know you more intimately than anyone else. I know who you are as a person. I know your dreams and goals, your fears and what makes you laugh." The rough pad of his thumb lightly skimmed back and forth over her knuckles, causing frissons of electricity to sizzle through her body. "And I know every inch of your beautiful body and have proven time and time again I know how to make it sing for me."

He was right; Tony did know all of those things about her. Their time spent together these last few months had included more pillow talk than most, for lack of a better term, friends-with-benefits arrangements.

Tony was more. *They* were more.

"So, long term? Yeah," he said, "I think the plan worked brilliantly. Though, I'll admit that I never dared to dream we'd ever get to this point. But now that we are, I don't know how I could have ever doubted it."

Trish drew her brows together as something sparked to life in the pit of her stomach and soured her gut in warning, but she couldn't imagine what it might be for. Bad news of some kind?

"Don't you feel like everything with us is somehow meant to be? Like no matter how far we stray from each other, our love will always bring us back together and we'd be exactly where we are right now."

Our love? "Tony, I..." She what? She had no clue how to finish that sentence.

"I'm making a mess out of this, aren't I?" He blew out a deep breath and framed her face with his free hand. "Trish, I'm trying to tell you that I love you."

Warning bells tolled in the back of her head now. She proceeded with care, hoping things weren't about to take a bad turn. "I love you too, Tony, you know that."

"No, I mean I am *in* love with you. Have been from the first time I saw you on that playground, and I haven't stopped since. I just never identified it as love before. People called it puppy love, a crush, a challenge. Some of my friends even called you my obsession. That one is probably the most honest out of all of them, but they're all still wrong, because what I've always felt for you is so much more than that. It's love, pure and simple, and unconditional."

With her heart racing, Trish slowly pushed herself up to a sitting position and he followed suit. *Shit. What is he doing? Why is he doing it?* Okay, deep breaths. "Tony, it's been a really long day for both of us. We should pack things up and head back."

He shook his head before she even finished talking. "Not yet. I'm through with denying myself any longer. We deserve more. We deserve to be together."

"I don't understand what this is all about. We're together all the time. I see you more than I see my sister, and I *live* with her."

"So why not live with me?"

Seconds dragged out as she stared. She needed to say something. Did she already say something? She couldn't remember. Hell, she couldn't remember what *he* said anymore. "Can you repeat that?"

"I said, so why not live with me." Then he held up a stunning diamond ring with antique details in the band. The precious stone in the middle winked at her in the moonlight. "Trish, I love you. I always have and I swear to you that I always will. I'll treat you like the amazing woman you are and I promise to lift you up when you're down and let you do the same for me. I want to spend the rest of my life with you. Marry me, T. Make me the happiest man alive."

Trish scrambled to her feet just as the panic attack hit her. "Are you joking? What on earth would make you think it's a good idea to propose marriage in something that's not even technically a relationship?"

Tony rose and stared at her like she'd gone crazy. He might not be far from the mark at the moment. "What do you mean not a relationship? Trish, we couldn't be in more of a relationship if we tried. We spend every minute of free time together, you stay at my place, we talk about the future, and what we have in the bedroom is fucking insane, if you'll excuse the pun."

"No, I will *not* excuse the pun." She had no idea why she said that other than she felt compelled to be contrary. She needed to end this. Right here, right now. She'd let things go too far and now it was too late to salvage anything. "Look, Tony, I love you as a person and a friend, and yes, we have insane chemistry in the bedroom, but that doesn't mean we should get *married* for fuck's sake. We never talked about this thing we had going getting more serious or taking things to the next level. There would have been a talk, and we never had a talk."

"We never had a talk about *anything*. Once we decided to start having a physical relationship, things happened organically just like all of them do. We agreed to keep things casual in the beginning, but we never said that it couldn't change or grow, so how was I supposed to know you wanted to have your cake and eat it too? Because that's exactly what this is. You want all the benefits of having me as your boyfriend with the freedom to think of me as your friendly fuck-buddy who's okay with walking away whenever you decide you're done."

"Jesus, Tony, I was with a man for almost a decade and had no idea just how wrong we were together. It's absolutely impossible to even fathom that after a few short months with you, I could fall in love and know in my heart of hearts that we're meant to be or even know that I want to spend the rest of my life with you. And I think if you're honest, you'll see that it's not possible from your end either."

"Don't patronize me the way that asshole used to do to you, Trish. You can't tell me that I don't know what I'm talking about. I know how I feel and I know that there's no reason for me to wait six months, a year, or five years to see if I'll still love you enough then to want to start my life with you. My love for you would only get stronger with time, not less. So if I say I'm ready now, then I'm ready."

"This is exactly why I wanted the no-beds rule," she said, her voice escalating. "Beds skew the level of intimacy and amplify feelings of lust into something they're not."

"That's a bunch of bullshit, but even if it wasn't, which of us was the one to call that rule off, Trish? Wasn't me."

She closed her eyes and prayed her legs would hold up for a little longer before buckling. "You're right. This is my fault, and I'm so sorry." She heard him scoff and looked up to see hurt twisting his gorgeous features. "I think it would be best if you took me home, Tony. And though I'm sure it goes without saying, this, whatever it is, has to be over. I didn't realize I'd misled you so strongly and I'm sorry if I've hurt you."

"Don't worry about me, T. I'm no longer your concern, apparently." He released a mirthless laugh that chilled her to the bone. "Maybe I'll go find a friend to screw around with for a while to help me get over you and hope I don't start to 'strongly mislead' her. Seems to have worked great for you."

If she'd had anything left of her heart after the breakup with Nick, Tony had effectively stripped it away with that statement. Not that he was wrong for saying it. She deserved that and more. So much more.

They didn't speak the rest of the night, not even when he dropped her off at Rhianna's. As a test to prove to herself that she wasn't in love with Tony, she watched him drive away and imagined that he wasn't going the meager two-minutes to his house, but rather some place far away where she'd never be able to see him again.

Immediately, she got sick, the contents of her stomach in the street just as vile as how she'd treated the man she loved. But no matter how they felt about each other, it wouldn't change her answer to the proposal. It was ludicrous to think she could find her Happily Ever After so soon, and in her hometown of all places, as if she'd never had to go farther than her front yard to find her soulmate. It wasn't logical or practical. He had to see that.

Either way, she needed to apologize to him for the way she treated him so callously. She'd beg his forgiveness and hopefully, in time, he wouldn't hate her.

CHAPTER SEVEN

Paddy's was fairly slow for a Saturday afternoon, but then again, it was Labor Day weekend. The last summer hurrah for families to get in a long-weekend mini-vacay with the kids before the new school year started the following week.

A handful of the die-hards still showed up for lunch, though, so Trish had been able to stay busy. Between the food and drink orders, restocking the bar, prepping enough garnishes for an entire week, and dusting every bottle of liquor and the shelves they sat on, she'd been well and truly distracted. And distractions were a necessity the past couple of weeks to keep her mind off the shambles she'd made of her life in such a short amount of time.

In April, she'd come home with her tail tucked between her legs and her heart crushed by the man she'd thought loved her. Now, a mere five months later, her tail was docked, and her heart felt shattered beyond repair. The current situation wasn't only different because it involved a different man, but also because the man wasn't at fault for her heartache. This time it'd been her own doing that caused the pain, both his and her own.

Heartache.

She scoffed at the word as she wiped the bar down for the third time in the last thirty minutes. Such a mild emotion for what she felt, and yet she didn't deserve to claim even that much for herself. Oh, she definitely deserved to be suffering, but not in the pure and blameless way of someone whose heart had been mishandled by another. She'd had that right five months ago. But not any more.

It killed her to know she'd hurt Tony. How did everything get so mixed up? Thinking back, she couldn't even pinpoint when things had crossed from a casual summer fling into the L-word territory, much less a place where marriage proposals were even on the horizon.

The night after his soccer game when they made love in his bed had been a clear game-changer. Before that they'd kept things hot and heavy and away from the intimacy of the bedroom. Those hours spent tangled up together, surrounded by the crisp scent of his sheets and the heavy musk of their love-making still glistening on their naked flesh...they'd been the most honest and beautiful hours of her life.

But if she was being honest with herself, she'd stopped seeing Tony as "a friend she had sex with" and started seeing him as "a lover she had an unbreakable friendship with" long before that. She'd simply been vigilant about not allowing herself to analyze any part of it. After all, how could it be true if she never realized the truth?

"That's some tree-falling-in-the-forest bullshit right there," she grumbled.

"Personally, I've always thought the trees don't actually fall when no one's around." Trish looked up to find Jason sitting on a stool in front of her with his perpetual dimpled smile that would have marked him as a rake from a mile away had he lived in Regency England. "Who wants to go through all that trouble without an audience, right?"

He reached over the bar and speared a green olive with a

toothpick, popping it into his mouth and chewing it with the same enthusiasm he seemed to do with everything. She offered him a weak smile. Pretending everything was coming up roses wasn't necessary around Jason, so she took advantage and gave her feigned contentment a rest.

"Hi, Jason. I'm surprised to see you. Aren't you reffing at the youth soccer tournament today with...?" Why she couldn't bring herself to say his name aloud was beyond her. Though, if she had to take a stab at a guess, it might have something to do with the fact he'd purposely stayed away from Paddy's and avoided her attempts to talk to him since she turned his proposal down.

"Nah, they had enough people to cover it, and I didn't feel like being in the sun for five hours straight."

"Can I get you something?"

"Usual," he answered, and she walked to the cooler and pulled out a Point. "So word on the street is you're shipping out to Chi-Town on Monday."

Trish paused for a moment, surprised. Popping the top for him, she set the bottle in front of him. "Yeah, I called my friend last week and told her I'd make a go of her dress shop with her. I've stayed here a lot longer than planned." She grabbed a couple dirty glasses and placed them in the sink. "It's time I move on with my life."

"You know that 'moving on with your life' and 'moving out of town' aren't mutually exclusive, right?" She stopped folding and refolding the damp bar towel and peeked up at him through her lashes. Jason gentled his voice and his expression turned serious for the first time around her. "You don't have to move *away* to move *on*, Trish."

Dropping the rag, she snorted. "There's nothing here for me, Jason. I can't make a career out of waitressing, and even if I miraculously had a desirable way of making a living, I could never stay here. I hate small town life, always have."

His blue eyes squinted in thought over the brown bottle as he tipped it up for a drink. "You sure about that? Because from the few months I've known you, I never would've guessed that for a minute. What I *have* seen is a woman who's comfortable in her surroundings and quick with a smile and warm hello to anyone she passes."

Trish sighed. "I appreciate what you're trying to do, Jason, but being comfortable in my hometown and friendly with its people doesn't mean I like living here."

"You're right, it doesn't," he admitted, sliding off his stool and heading to a table recently abandoned by customers. He gathered the glasses together and started carrying them to the bar. "I could prove my point with more detailed examples."

Trish took the glasses he'd bussed and started dunking them in the soapy water while watching him go back for more dishes. What a brat. He'd dropped that line knowing full well she'd bite. Sweeping a quick look at the three tables currently occupied to make sure no one appeared to need anything, she braced her hands on the edge of the sturdy oak counter and narrowed her eyes at the man returning with the rest of the stuff from the table.

"Okay, I give. Tell me these supposed detailed examples you have."

He smiled, showing off his dimples. "Curiosity get the better of you?"

"Honestly, I don't think you have anything, so I'm calling your bluff."

Jason clapped his hands once and rubbed them together in anticipation. Then he mirrored her stance, gripping the edge of the bar, and began giving her an account of events like a computer spitting out data.

"Shortly after you moved back home, you overheard one of your customers talking about how she wouldn't be able to plant flowers around her house this year due to the surgery she was scheduled to have on both wrists. You could've ignored it, after all she wasn't talking to you, but instead you approached her and offered to plant well over two hundred tiny annuals in her flower beds and then also ended up weeding and cutting her grass on your free day from work. From what I heard, Mrs. Beran was so thankful that she sent you a lovely card and a gift certificate from the Chamber of Commerce, which you then spent treating the Shark Bytes to a post-game treat at Frosty Freeze."

Trish's mouth gaped as she stared at him.

"How about the fact that you took your niece and nephew to see every performance that came to the high school. A Capella groups, musicals, the hypnotist dude, comedy shows, and whatever else they booked there over the summer. You also made dates with each of them on separate weeks for some one-on-one time.

"Then there's the kid sporting events. You asked Erin to work around your nephew's baseball games and made sure you were front row for every game, shouting and cheering louder than anyone else in the bleachers. On the days you didn't have to work during Tony's kids' games and even Tony's games, you made every one of those, too. You didn't choose to be somewhere else, and you can't even say you attended out of kindness because you got into those games every bit as much as the parents.

"Shall I go on?" he asked with a cocky arch of his brow. "Because I can. For quite a while. I haven't even gotten to July yet."

Still in shock, Trish shook her head. Small town gossip was one thing, but this was ridiculous. "That's creepy, Jason. How do you know all that?"

"Well..." Glancing over his shoulder at the customers behind him, he made sure no one was eavesdropping. "Unlike you, I haven't been distracted by a partner to share my bed with, and that gives me time to notice *everything* around me. I'm a carefree, flirtatious joker—to a fault—but not even a blind man could miss how happy you've been since you've been here."

"And no one ever suspects the Good Time Charlie to be

paying attention," she said in awe. His smile now beamed back at her, framed by his dimples.

Trish speared her hair with her fingers, trying to wrap her mind around everything she'd just heard and the idea that apparently there's plenty more. Suddenly she felt stifled and a dull ache started pulsing in her temples. "I, um—" She cleared her throat. "I need some air. Can you...?"

Jason jerked his head in the direction of the door. "I'll cover you. Take your time." She didn't waste a second skirting around the end of the counter. "Hey," he said, catching her arm before she could pass him. She met his eyes and saw true concern. "I'm sorry if I upset you. You know that's not my intention, right?"

Covering his hand with hers, Trish gave him a light squeeze and an understanding nod before walking briskly to the front entrance. It wasn't until she stepped from the air-conditioned pub into the oppressing humidity outside that she could finally drag air into her lungs.

She moved to the corner of the building and leaned back against the bricks. Tilting her face to the sun, Trish closed her eyes and focused on taking slow, deep breaths. In the wake of everything Jason recounted, she couldn't continue to claim she hated small town life, or at least not in Fort Atkinson. Thinking back on how she spent her summer, she was helpless to stop the smile—the first real one in weeks—that reflected the emotions rising inside her.

How had she not realized before now? She'd truly been happy the past few months. Sure, the town had a gossip mill the size of Texas, and everyone at some point found themselves smack in the middle of it. But it was in that same manner that the community heard about others in need and then banded together to form a network of support and help.

A part of her would miss the excitement of the big city where the entertainment options were endless and the billboards lit up the streets at night like a Technicolor version of the day. But it wasn't as though she was locked within the walls of Fort like some townie prisoner. If she wanted big city options, there were plenty within driving distance.

Beyond that, her little town had a lot of things to offer that weren't possible when she lived in New York. Things like the outdoor theater on the outskirts of town where the bed of a truck easily transformed into an actual bed for a double feature movie date under the stars.

God, the *stars*. They were nothing short of magnificent on a clear night. Trish had always loved lying on her back in the soft grass, ankles crossed and hands folded over her stomach, as she searched for the constellations she knew of and made up names and stories for the ones she didn't.

Thankfully, light pollution hadn't tainted their little corner of the world. A dull orange cast over New York City like a dome, separating it from the rest of the universe, and had always made her wistful. The only orange glow out here belonged to the sunset, its bright streak painted over the horizon, bleeding into slashes of pink, purple, and red. Then, at dusk, the fireflies blinked on and off, challenging the kids—or the big kids at heart —to play the old-as-time game of catch and release. As night wore on, they grew more and more scarce until finally turning the evening over to the brilliance of the stars overhead.

Damn it. She *did* love it here. But even so, she couldn't stay. One of the small town drawbacks was seeing people you knew no matter where you went. With as involved as Tony was in the community, she was guaranteed to be in the same place at the same time as him, and with everything she'd already put him through, she'd not make him uncomfortable in his own town. So, to that end, her plan for moving to Chicago in two days was still a go. But now she'd be doing it with the knowledge that she'd rather stay. Too bad she didn't have anything worth staying for.

"Trish?"

Oh, no. No-no-no-no-no! With her eyes still closed, she

squeezed them tight and prayed like hell. *Please, dear God, let this be a bad dream. Turn it into a nightmare if you want, just please don't let it be real.*

"It is you." The man's voice she knew almost better than her own couldn't have been more than a few feet away. Then she felt a shadow fall over her and she knew it was no dream, good, bad, or otherwise. This was really happening.

Reluctantly, Trish opened her eyes to find Nick standing before her. His face lit up with obvious joy at having found her, though why he was looking in the first place she couldn't imagine.

"Jesus, Nick, what the hell are you doing here?"

A brief wince interrupted his happiness. "I suppose I deserve that."

She barked out a humorless laugh. "You *suppose* you deserve that? Are you fucking kidding me?" Trish pushed off the building to stand tall and revel in the anger now coursing through her like lightning. "Over nine years together and you never *once* came with me to see my hometown or meet my family and friends. But almost six months *after* you break up with me and send me packing halfway across the country you decide, what, to take a quick trip out to say 'hi' for old times' sake?"

"Yes. I mean, no, I didn't come all the way out here just to say 'hi', obviously," Nick said with a tinge of irritation. "That'd be a little extreme, don't you think?"

"I'm thinking a whole lot of things right now, but I doubt you'd want me to voice any of them." Trish crossed her arms over her chest in an attempt to appear bigger or stronger. That's what cornered animals did, all while trembling on the inside from anxiety and fear of the unknown. "So why don't you tell me why you *are* here, Nick, and then you can go back to New York where you belong."

He expelled a heavy sigh and rubbed the back of his neck, something he did when he needed a few moments to gather his thoughts before speaking. Finally, he steepled his hands and rested his fingers on his mouth as he studied her, probably looking for her fleshy underbelly where he could strike her down with the least amount of effort. Well, she'd be damned if she'd show him anything. As far as he was concerned, she was covered from head to toe in thick, impenetrable scales. *Good luck, asshole.*

"I've reconsidered our situation. Almost a decade of life together is too much to throw away because of some minor differences in what we want." Nick took a deep breath, carefully lowered to one knee—wincing upon contact, she knew, from the idea of his designer dress slacks touching a dirty sidewalk—then retrieved a ring box from his pocket and held it up as he snapped it open. "Trish Lynn Howell, will you do me the great honor of being my wife?"

She must be getting Punk'd. It was the only explanation, because this was the most fucked up shit she could think of happening. For years, her greatest desire was to be engaged to a man she loved and start the next chapter of their life together. Now she had two proposals in as many weeks that she *didn't* want, and in two days, she planned on moving to Chicago to start a new and very *non*-affianced life.

What. The. Fuck.

"What do you say, Trishy?" Standing up, he thoroughly brushed off the knee of his pants before straightening and giving her his attention. "Let's go home. I took care of your flight. All you need is an overnight bag, and we'll have what little is left of your things shipped back."

When she finally opened her mouth to speak, the lack of emotion—either good or bad—surprised her. Her words were robotic, matter-of-fact. "I've always hated it when you call me that."

Turning away from him, Trish walked back into the bar and went to check on the three tables of customers that remained. They'd been done with their food for some time, but they were regulars who enjoyed getting together once a week for a couple hours so she knew they wouldn't be in any hurry to leave.

"Ladies, can I get you anything or has the handsome Mr. Jason been attending your needs during my break?"

A streak of sunlight shone into the bar and vanished as Nick opened the pub door and moved directly behind her, speaking as though she hadn't just asked her customers a question that he'd be interrupting. "I thought you loved that nickname I gave you. I used it all the time and you never said anything."

She pointedly ignored him and waited for the group of women who'd been discussing their gardens—one of which was none other than Mrs. Madsen—to answer her. Unfortunately, the gossip mongers homed in on the *Young and the Exes* mini-soap and forgot all about refills. Before any of them had a chance to ask the burning questions Trish knew balanced on the tips of their tongues, she quickly said, "Okay, just give me a holler if you need anything."

As she grabbed a few dirty dishes on her way to the bar, she answered Nick without bothering to offer eye contact. "I hated it. It sounded like I was a baby, which in retrospect I suppose is appropriate considering that's how you treated me."

Nick sputtered as he trailed behind her. "What the hell are you talking about? I never treated you like a baby."

Trish rounded the counter and handed the dishes off to Jason. "On the contrary, Nick. You always patronized me and did things for me without asking. You ordered my food and drinks in restaurants whenever we went out with other people; I wasn't allowed to balance my own checkbook or pay my own bills. You treated me like I didn't have the sense God gave me to make any decisions that might actually matter or that might embarrass you in front of our friends."

Jason sidled up close to her with his body turned slightly into hers as he stared at Nick through steely blue eyes. She'd never seen Jason like this before. Gone was the flirtatious man ready with a quick smile and playfully inappropriate compliment. In his place stood an intimidating man with his over-six-foot athletic build and muscular arms folded over his broad chest, stretching his black Fort Atkinson Blackhawk Football T-shirt to max capacity. "There a problem here, sweetheart?"

"No problem, Jason," she said easily. "My ex just wanted to stop in and propose, but now he's leaving to head back to New York, aren't you, Nick?"

She wouldn't have thought it possible, but she felt Jason tense even more beside her. "Your ex?" He said the words as one might say "putrid waste." Then he clearly directed the next part at said waste. "Don't let the heavy door castrate you on the way out. Or do. Whatever."

Nick returned Jason's glare. "Sweetheart?" he practically sneered. "After everything we had, Trish, I can't believe you moved on so easily. Especially with some small town jock who sticks around to relive his glory days in order to feel like he's worth something."

Trish flattened a palm against Jason's chest just as he'd lowered his arms and likely prepared to launch over the bar. Then she leaned in and hissed, "Goddammit, Nick, you can insult me all you want, but you don't get to come to *my home* and insult *my friends*." Without taking her eyes from Nick, she said, "Jason, please give me a minute."

"I don't think—"

"*Jason.*"

"Fuck. Tony's gonna have my balls for this," he grumbled. "I'll be right over there if you need me."

Jason had directed his last statement to Trish, but it was obvious it'd been a warning meant for Nick. Regardless, she wouldn't need his help. For the first time in almost ten years, Trish saw her ex-boyfriend clearly, and she was confident on how to handle him.

"Nick, who I'm dating or even *whether* I'm dating, is no longer your concern. Just as who you may or may not be dating is none of mine. I'm sorry you came all this way for nothing, but it's time for you to go."

"You're not even going to let me state my case?"

She sighed. Even marriage proposals were treated as possible business mergers where he thought it was possible to win-over the other party. If letting him try and fail was the only way to get rid of him, so be it. "Fine. State your case, and *then* you can go."

Nick's face soured. "I don't like that you've already made up your mind that you won't like what I have to say."

She shrugged and began the task of removing glasses from the soapy sink and dunking them into the sanitizer. "Then you know where the door is."

"Okay, I get it," he said hastily, holding his hands up like white flags. "Trishy—I mean, *Trish*, I've done a lot of thinking during our separation. I realize now that feeling like I needed to stay in the neighborhood where I grew up was a case of cold feet, not to mention unfair."

She cocked a hip out and crossed her arms. "And selfish."

He offered her a clipped nod, not thrilled at her interjection. "My point is, there's no reason we can't compromise and find an area we like that has houses instead of apartments. Then we both have what we want and we're both happy."

Trish couldn't help it. She laughed. "You don't get it, Nick. I didn't just want a house. I wanted us to raise our family in a house outside of the city. Something with a big yard where our kids could play and grow and we could enjoy barbeques with our friends. Houses in the city have front stoops that lead to sidewalks and there's no room for kids to play or to put a grill out."

He frowned. "I don't even know how to grill. Why is that so important to you?"

"We come from two different worlds, and in the beginning, I wanted the same kind of life you did. I loved the excitement of the city and everything it offered. But somewhere along the line that changed, and when we talked about our future, I thought you had changed along with me."

A sense of utter calm flowed through her as an epiphany rose out from the mist of confusion she'd been roaming aimlessly in for the last several months. "You're nothing of what I need in a partner, Nick. And if you take a close look at me, at who I've become, you'll realize I'm no longer the one for you either. I need a man who loves to laugh with me, who loves to be with me no matter what we're doing. Who *loves* me just as I am, unapologetically and unconditionally. Can you honestly say that man is you?"

Nick swallowed and replaced the ring box in his pocket as he studied her. Finally, he spoke. "I'm sorry for any pain I caused you, Trish. I wish you nothing but happiness in your future." He gave her a wan smile. "I hope he knows how lucky he is to have you."

That wasn't the problem. It was that Tony didn't know how lucky Trish knew *she* was to have *him*. He'd been going through the last two weeks thinking she didn't want him—due to her own cowardice and stupidity—and that ate at her like nothing else.

"Thank you, Nick."

Glancing quickly over at Jason and then back to her, Nick gave her a curt nod and walked out of Paddy's. As soon as the door closed, her knees sagged. She braced her forearms on the bar and rested her head on top of them as she took deep breaths to settle her nerves. A smattering of applause broke out in the room, and she lifted her head to find her customers—her fellow friends and neighbors—clapping their approval.

Trish blushed and straightened, using a menu to fan herself from the heat of the emotional roller coaster she'd just ridden.

Mrs. Madsen spoke up. "Well, my dear, what are you waiting for? One proposal down, one to go, wouldn't you say?"

Had this been New York, Trish would've wondered if the woman was psychic or preternaturally intuitive. But this was Fort

Atkinson, where everyone knew everyone and it was a wonderful thing. Mrs. Madsen wasn't psychic. She was in-the-know and wanted their happiness. And also maybe a little more juice to add to the story she'd get to tell later as being an eye-witness to the incredible event. Such was the way of life in her small hometown, and she knew she'd never want it any other way.

Trish faced the man still behind the bar with her. "Jason?"

"I've got you covered and I'll call Erin to give her a heads up."

"Shit," she said, "I'll have to call Rhi for a ride."

"Take mine," Jason said, placing keys her in hand. "Now, go, get the hell out of here."

"Thank you," she rushed out before smacking a big kiss on his cheek. Then she grabbed her purse from under the bar and ran out the door to the cheers of her customers.

As she got into Jason's car she tried to suppress her nerves throwing a fucking rave in her stomach. If she couldn't get them to settle down, she'd be paying for Jason's car to be cleaned and detailed. But it would all be worth it if things went her way.

If Tony could forgive her and give her the chance to make things right.

CHAPTER EIGHT

Tony walked up and down the sidelines of the soccer field, yelling out encouragement and instructions to his team. The former was always well received with toothless smiles, enthusiastic waves, or a quick thumbs up. The latter was an exercise in futility since the kids always followed the ball no matter what position they played. But as far as futile exercises went, it was one he gladly repeated week after week, year after year.

This was the last game of the tournament, and miraculously, the Shark Bytes were tied for first with the Mighty Minnows. Whichever team won this game took first place for the season. Not that the kids cared all that much. They just loved playing and hearing their families cheering for them. One of the reasons he loved coaching kids at this age was because he envied their simplistic outlook on life. As long as something was fun, it was worth doing. If they loved someone, they showed it without ulterior motives.

If only it were that simple for adults. Then maybe the last two weeks would have been spent showing Trish how much he loved her instead of trying to bury that love so deep that it suffocated and stopped hurting so goddamn much. But, if anything, he hurt more today than he did yesterday and the day before that.

"Scottie," he yelled through cupped hands. "You can pick flowers for Jessica *after* the game! Watch the ball, little man!"

Scottie looked at the fistful of yellow weeds in his hand and then back to Tony. His face scrunched up into newfound determination, tossed the stuff over his shoulder, and hunkered down into position.

And in another five minutes, Tony would find the boy picking weeds all over again. Because girls made guys go crazy until they couldn't focus on anything but how to make the fairer sex happy, whether at the age of five or fifty-five. Dandelions probably wouldn't have helped, but Tony wondered if he could have done or said anything differently that would've made Trish reconsider rejecting him and his love.

"Tony, I need to talk to you."

Every muscle in his body snapped tight at the sound of Trish's voice and her breaths sawing in and out like she'd just ran a marathon. Without turning to look at her, he yelled out to tell Austin to stop playing with a caterpillar and run down the field with the rest of the kids. He didn't drop his fuzzy new pet, but ran toward his teammates and even managed to kick the ball with it still on his hand. Tony counted that as a victory.

"I'm a little busy right now, Trish," he said. "If you still want to talk later, give me a call."

"I've tried calling several dozen times. You don't answer them."

He was torn. Just having her here with him made him feel the most complete he had in weeks, and he wanted to kiss her senseless. On the other hand, she'd ran the moment he leveled with her about the depth of his feelings. His heart couldn't survive being discarded again. He settled on shrugging and moving down the field to follow the action. He felt her keeping pace with him and caught himself slowing so she didn't have to run alongside him.

"So this time I'll answer." Maybe, he amended silently. He wanted it all with her. If she offered him anything less, it would only make it that much harder to heal. Which is why he'd adopted the all-or-nothing mentality for the first time ever when it came to Trish. But it was necessary if he wanted to move the fuck on with his life.

"I don't blame you, but I also don't believe you, and I really need to talk to you."

"You'll have to wait until after the game." Tony raked his hands through his hair in frustration. "Honestly, I'm not sure I'll want to talk then either. It's been a long damn day and I won't have it in me." Tony planted his feet and crossed his arms over his chest, hoping he portrayed some kind of fierce statue that lacked emotion. Like a big ugly gargoyle. He bet gargoyles didn't have women problems. "Tomorrow would be better."

"How can I believe you'll want to talk to me tomorrow when you can't even *look* at me today?"

Tony ground his back molars together making his jaw muscles tic in irritation. Slowly, he turned only his head and peered down at her standing next to him. How was it possible she was even more beautiful than he remembered her? *Because life's a cruel bitch with a sick sense of humor.*

He arched an eyebrow. "Satisfied?"

She shook her head, but he didn't think it was in answer to his question. It seemed like a frustrated shake, like she couldn't figure out what to do next. "Just promise me that we'll talk after the game and I'll go wait on the bleachers."

Pools of moisture appeared to be collecting in her dark chocolate eyes, but it didn't make sense. She was the one who turned him down, who broke things off between them. There'd be no reason for her to be upset, much less cry.

Unless she misses the sex and wants things to go back to the way they were in the beginning. Hell, he'd been the one to give her a sexual awakening. Maybe she's afraid she'll go back to being "broken" if she's with anyone else. Then a dark thought seeped in, tainting his perfect memories of her and made him murderous. *Maybe she'd already tried being with someone else and he hadn't been able to make her come like he did. Christ.*

"Can't make that promise, Trish," he gritted out. "I think it's best you go home."

"Okay, but remember, you're not leaving me a choice."

Whatever. The last time he'd given her a choice, she given the wrong—

"Trish, what the hell are you doing?" He watched in shock as she stalked into the middle of the field where the kids amassed around the ball. "Get off the field, T, I'm serious!"

Trish Howell continued her journey, head held high, shoulders thrown back, and hands fisted at her sides. He heard everything go to hell around him as his eyes stayed glued to her retreating back. Parents started talking and speculating amongst themselves in the bleachers. The kids from his team caught on to what was happening and ran to her like she was handing out giant pixie sticks. A ref's whistle blew to stop the game—not that he had any players left actively participating—and raised his hands in question to Tony.

Yeah, like Tony had any clue as to how to deal with the current clusterfuck his championship game had turned into. Erin, who'd been watching her niece play, appeared at his side.

"What's Trish doing on the field?"

He shook his head. "No fucking idea."

"She's supposed to be at Paddy's. Jason called me and told me he's covering for her, but he didn't say why."

He'd noticed Trish wore her dark green uniform T-shirt with skinny jeans and a pair of worn cowboy boots that had probably never stepped foot in a pasture, but he'd assumed she was ready to work later in the day. It never occurred to him that she'd leave in the middle of her shift. What the hell was going on?

"Stay here, will you?" he asked Erin. "I'm going to send the kids back to the sidelines while I deal with her."

"Yeah, no problem." He stepped over the line of white-painted grass, but Erin stopped him from going any farther with a gentle hand on his arm. "Go easy on her. I know you're hurting, Tony, but so is she. Remember that."

A thin layer of his anger slipped away at her reminder. Tony hadn't seen Trish since she turned him down, but Erin had. This was her way of letting him know that Trish hadn't walked away from them completely unscathed. He gave his friend a sharp nod and then followed the same path Trish had blazed a minute before.

After sending both teams back to the sidelines, Tony looked over at the other coach and the referee who were both looking to him for some sort of idea as to what the plan was. Trish stood center field, her solemn gaze on him. He almost rolled his eyes, but instead made his hands into a "T" to signal for a break. The ref blew the whistle again and yelled, "Time out," though Tony didn't know whose benefit it was for. Everyone in a three block radius already seemed to have taken a time out so they could watch the drama unfold. Perfect.

He turned his attention to the woman causing the unholy uproar. A light breeze picked up strands of her long hair and carried them to the side. His fingers itched to reach up and tuck them back where they belonged for the sole excuse to feel the silkiness on his skin.

"What's all this about, Trish? What's so important it can't wait?"

"You," she said softly. "You're what's so important, Tony. And I've wasted two whole weeks letting you think otherwise. Letting *myself* think otherwise. But the truth is that of all the people in my life, it's you who means the most to me."

"That's great, Trish," he said, tinged in sarcasm. "Knowing I'm the most important person in your life is going to help me sleep a lot better at night. Now let's go." He reached for her arm, but she took a step back.

"No, that's not what I'm trying to say." Her brows drew together and she used both hands to push her hair back and pull it over one shoulder. "I'm trying to tell you that I love you, Tony. As in, I am *in love with you*. Body, heart, and soul."

Tony froze. Not that he'd been moving. He wasn't going to force his presence on Trish a moment more, even to throw her over his shoulder and remove her from the field. But it still felt like whatever else he didn't have control over—the hairs on his arms, the blood in his veins, the air in his lungs, the beat of his heart—froze in time.

Then her words from the other week came back to him, and the burning embers of the fire that razed his heart to the ground caught fire again and took him from freezing to boiling in seconds.

"You'll have to forgive me, but I'm finding this declaration a little hard to believe. Not two weeks ago you told me that falling in love and knowing you're meant to spend a lifetime with someone is impossible in only a few short months."

"I was wrong," she said simply, her voice cracking with emotion. "Time and experience has nothing to do with it. I realize that now. It's how the person makes you feel. About yourself, about life, all of it. You make me feel like the most beautiful and precious woman in the world, like I can do anything I set my mind on. All without even trying because it's simply who you are."

Tears spilled over her cheeks, but she dashed them away with her fingers, clearly not wanting to appear weak in such a vulnerable state. Forever his strong girl, his Trish.

"Sometimes," she whispered, "all it takes is a glance from you, and my heart swells with so much love that I can hardly draw my next breath. But I kept telling myself that it had to be lust or infatuation, because I couldn't handle knowing that what we have was more real, more genuine, than anything before. "

He dug his fingers into his palms to keep himself from reaching out to her. His body and heart and mind were in a goddamn Mexican standoff, all pointing weapons at the other two while shouting their demands on how to handle the situation.

Body: take her, mark her, and fuck her until she knows who she belongs to, now and forever. Heart: forgive her, hold her, and make love to her until she feels secure in their love. Mind: start over, go slow, and see how things progress from there.

No doubt about it, Tony wanted to listen to his body and heart a hell of a lot more than his mind. But following each of them, first his body and then his heart, is what got him into this mess in the first place. The logical solution was to try the third option and hope like hell it had better results than the other two.

"Trish," he began, swallowing hard, "you already know how much I love you. For you to finally tell me you feel the same makes me happier than I have words to explain. And part of me wants to pull you into my arms and forget the last two weeks ever happened. But I don't think it's a good idea."

More tears overflowed from her eyes, but she didn't bother to wipe away their evidence. Her teeth bore down on her trembling lip until its pink flesh blanched to white. It was another valiant attempt to not break down, and another stake driven through his chest.

He cleared his voice when it didn't immediately work. "I'm not saying there's no chance. We can start over and take things slow. Let them progress naturally instead of starting in the middle only to find ourselves at the end without any of the beginning stuff. I don't want to take the chance of picking up where we left off because you're afraid of losing me now, and then realizing weeks or months later that you're not sure about us. Do you understand?"

Trish gave him a sad smile. "Yes, I understand."

"You sure?"

She nodded. "Absolutely. I get it."

"Good. We can talk more about everything later, including how to make things work around you living two hours away in Chicago. But for now, let's give the gossip mill a rest and see who wins the game, okay?"

The knots in Tony's stomach loosened somewhat when she offered him a real smile. It was a start, but he didn't trust himself to touch her yet, so he turned and started making his way off the field. He kept his sights on the kids and their puzzled expressions, too much of a pussy to make eye contact with the adults looking on in eerie silence.

"Ask me again," her strong voice called to him from behind, stopping him in his tracks.

He closed his eyes and took a deep breath, wishing he remembered how that Serenity Prayer went. Maybe it only mattered that he knew he needed to ask for strength and patience, who the hell knew. Tony didn't know how long he stood there, but he heard her come up on his left, and from the sound of her voice, she faced him.

"Please," she said. "Ask me again."

Sighing, he opened his eyes and turned toward her. "Trish, I don't know what you're—" She tucked her fingers into one of her front pockets and pulled out his grandmother's ring. "How did you get that?"

"I stopped at your place on the way here to get it, because while I understand your point about us skipping over all the beginning stuff and it being a good idea to start fresh and try again, I don't agree with it."

"You don't—" Tony let out a frustrated chuckle as he rubbed his hands vigorously over his face a few times and then placed them on his hips to study her. In his peripheral vision, he saw hundreds of eyes on them, and now that they were a mere dozen feet from the edge of the field, everything they said could also be heard. Fuck it. If she didn't care about the spectacle they were making, then neither did he. "You don't agree with it? Mind telling me why?"

Trish took a single step forward. "We may not have started our relationship in the most traditional way, but that doesn't mean we skipped anything. The beginning is when you learn things about each other, what they like and dislike. Whether you're companionable and can survive the times when they're at their worst and still care for them.

"Tony, we've been doing that since the third grade. The first thing you learned about me was to never steal my softball glove. And I learned that if I don't want you to do something again, all I have to do is kick you in the shin."

She bit the inside of her cheek to hide her smirk, but it didn't do much good. Their audience snickered with a few of the younger members laughing at their coach for trying such a thing. But Tony couldn't keep a partial grin from creeping onto his face, either, so he supposed he'd forgive the little rascals.

"For the record, I wouldn't recommend that method of persuasion at this age," he said with a single brow cocked in challenge.

"Duly noted," she quipped. Then after a beat, she sobered and so did the conversation. "I was wrong two weeks ago, Tony, and I'll regret the things I said to you that day for the rest of my life. Your proposal was perfect, *everything* had been perfect, and I ruined all of it." She swallowed thickly and her brown eyes watered again. "But the worst part of it all...is thinking that I may have ruined any chance of there being an 'us' in the process."

Before he could answer or sweep her up into his arms to reassure her that he could never give up hope for them, she rocked down to her knees in front of him. The murmurs from the peanut

gallery swelled to above a whisper, but he didn't pay any attention. He was too stunned that the woman he loved and would do
anything for was on her knees holding up his grandmother's
wedding ring in both hands.

"Anthony Joseph DiAngelo, I love you with everything that I
am and everything I ever hope to be. I swear to you that I've never
been more sure of anything in my life and there won't be a day
that goes by that you'll regret this moment..." She took a deep
breath, exhaled, and then said, "...if only you'll find it in your
heart to ask me again."

Her words couldn't have been more perfect. They could have
been her wedding vows instead of merely a request that he
propose to her again. This woman was all he'd ever want in this
world, and nothing could keep him from granting her this wish
and every wish she'd ever have in the future.

Tony felt his hand shake as he reached for the ring, so he
curled it into a fist, inhaled deeply and got control over his body
before trying again. When he held the ring, he lowered himself to
his knees, then lower to sit on his heels so she at least had about
an inch in height on him to make it somewhat proper. However,
he didn't want to draw anything out. He'd already told her everything during the last proposal. Now it was time for simple and
quick, so he could let his body and heart make good on their
plans as soon as humanly possible.

Gazing into her warm brown eyes, Tony held her left hand in
his and did as he'd been ordered. "Will you marry me, baby?"

She beamed at him a moment before throwing her arms
around his neck and capturing his mouth for a kiss he happily
returned, trying to remember to keep it PG for the spectators he
could hear squealing in girlish delight and alternately pretending
to puke and gag and warn their coach of cooties.

Tony forced himself to pull away from his new fiancée so he
could place the ring on her finger and help her to stand. In
seconds, they were surrounded by the horde as hugs and well

wishes were offered for at least another half hour before things settled enough for the game to resume. Their coach's engagement must have wound up the Shark Bytes, because they ended up winning 5-1 in the highest scoring youth soccer game to date.

All in all, it'd turned out to be a pretty great day, and if Tony had anything to say about it, things would only get better from here on out. It was hard to imagine their future any other way with how fortunate they were. He loved his teaching career, and he'd always coach in the youth programs. Trish was a born entrepreneur and missed the business she'd worked so hard to grow back in New York, so it was only a matter of time before she did it again. But he also knew that he needed to let her come to that decision on her own, so he'd wait it out.

As everyone snapped pictures of the team with the trophy as tall as the champions who'd earned it, Tony pulled Trish behind the bleachers and stole a proper kiss filled with all the passion and love he held for his bride-to-be. Damn, that sounded good. It sounded *right*.

"You know," he said, looking on at the kids celebrating and oblivious to their coach's sudden disappearance, "we *are* at the fields a block from my place. I bet no one would notice if we slipped away to go do some celebrating of our own. I'll give you a ten-second head start since you're wearing boots."

Trish laughed, but shook her head. "No way. You can suck it up and wait until later."

"Oh, sweetheart, I thought you would have learned by now not to challenge me. Ten...nine..."

"Tony, damn it, stop."

"...seven..."

She started to back away from him. "I'm not kidding." But she laughed and kept backing up.

"Better hurry," he said in a low voice with a smirk on his lips. "You remember what happened last time I caught you."

Her eyes flying wide, she gasped. "It's *daylight*."

He gave her a predatory smile that told her just how little he cared. "...four..."

"Shit!" she squeaked on a laugh before spinning and bolting down the road.

Tony counted the last two numbers in his head and took the couple seconds to enjoy watching her run from him. He wasn't really in a hurry. After all, they had the rest of their lives ahead of them to do everything from make love to discover new facets of their relationship. And they'd do all of it together.

She was his perfect game. They were a team, and when they had kids—fingers crossed she wanted enough to fill a soccer roster—they'd be an even bigger team.

"Ready or not, world," he said to himself as he started walking home, "here we come."

EPILOGUE

even months later...

S Trish sat on the edge of the bathtub and reflected on how different her life was from only a year ago. So much had happened in the short time since the day of their crazy shared proposal at the youth soccer tournament; sometimes she had a hard time believing it wasn't all a dream.

Tony hadn't wanted a long engagement, and she'd been more than happy to oblige. That was until she was in the middle of planning a wedding with only six months to prepare. Then she wanted to pull her hair out in great chunks, never speak to another relative for as long as she lived, and elope. But with some help from friends, everything came together beautifully, and they'd gotten married a little over a month ago.

Trish never imagined she could be so happy in love, and now that she was, she didn't think it was possible for that feeling to get any bigger. But staring at the two pink lines in the tiny window of the stick she held her hands, her heart already started swelling. Apparently she hadn't gotten any better at predicting how love worked.

Smiling, she stood and checked her reflection in the mirror

and removed the smudges of eyeliner from her mini-emotional bout when that second line came through. She composed herself to look as casual and unexcited as possible and exited the bathroom off of their living room.

"Come on, babe, hurry up," Tony said from his spot on the couch. His eyes were glued to the television, game controller in hand, and the eerie sounds of the horror video game echoing in the small space. "I need my navigator. I've got myself all turned around and can't remember how to get the hell out of here."

Concealing the pregnancy test, she sat in her spot next to him and looked at his character roaming around aimlessly. She loved their game nights where he worked the controller (she sucked at that part) and she acted as the backseat player. Her only requirement was that the game had to have a good storyline, not just constant shoot-em-up stuff. "You're in the library, so get out of there, take a left, two rights, and the exit will be straight ahead."

He leaned over and gave her a loud smack on the cheek. "How I ever finished any games without you is beyond me."

"Agreed," she said and watched as he followed her instructions. "Hey, remember that time a couple weeks ago when I was throwing up a lot for like a week?"

Tony turned to study her face, his brows drawn with concern. "Are you feeling sick again?"

"No, I feel great, actually."

"Oh, good," he said, returning to the game. "Yeah, I remember it. Why?" The character on the TV exited the building. "Finally," he muttered.

"Do you remember what you asked me toward the end?"

He winced as he continued to play the game. "I *may* have gotten a little excited and asked if you were pregnant."

Trish felt a flurry of butterfly wings in her belly. Placing a hand over her abdomen, it finally hit her that someday soon she'd be feeling flutters in there for real...from Tony's baby. *Their* baby.

Eyes glistening anew, she took a breath and said, "Ask me again."

His thumbs froze over the controller and the game character fidgeted in place. Tony's eyes locked onto hers. "What'd you say?"

Her smile broke wide. "I said ask me again."

"Trish, are you serious? We're going to have a baby?"

She nodded, causing her tears to run down her cheeks, and she handed him the plastic test. "We're going to have a baby."

Tony cheered as he picked her up to swing her around in the middle of the living room, controller tossed aside and game forgotten. She laughed and squealed when they fell back onto the couch. He apologized and made a big deal about needing to be more careful with her. She tried assuring him she wasn't going to break, but he wouldn't stop arguing about her "fragile state."

Funny how removing her shirt to reveal her naked breasts shut him up like pressing MUTE on a TV remote. "That's better," she said. "Now, if you're smart, you'll stop talking and start touching. After all, in less than nine months these puppies will be working overtime for our baby so you'll have limited visitation."

His eyes grew wide. "Limited visi— That's it, come here." Tony ducked his shoulder and hefted her up like a sack of potatoes, ignoring her commands to set her down as he stalked down the hall to their bedroom. "No use struggling, sweetheart. You've convinced me that I need to take advantage of having you all to myself before we're invaded. How does spending the next nine months in bed practicing how to make baby number two sound?"

Tony placed her in the center of the bed and followed her down to cover her with his body. Wrapping her arms around him, she pretended to think about it, then said, "I don't know. We'll consider this a test run. Show me what you've got...then ask me again."

ASK ME AGAIN is a stand-alone novella loosely based on Gina's youngest sister, Tricia, and her husband TJ, and was written as a cheap gift for their wedding on May 30th, 2015. Of course, Gina's kidding about the cheap gift part. (Maybe) The couple is still living out their HEA with their two sons, Matteo and Giovanni, both of whom Auntie GiGi spoils rotten.

Tricia and TJ

ACKNOWLEDGMENTS

As always, huge thanks to my husband and children who put up with my crazy schedules and neurotic behavior when I'm in the writing cave. Without their constant support and understanding, I wouldn't be able to do what I do.

To my sister and her husband who, when I asked, "What would you guys say to me writing a book based on your story," said, "Go for it!" and didn't care what I added or embellished in the name of good fiction. Thanks for being such great sports!

To Brenda Novak who created the original opportunity for this book when she invited me to be included in a box set to help raise money for finding a cure to diabetes. Thank you for being so sweet and patient with me and giving me the honor of helping such a worthy cause. I'm so grateful to have gotten to know you through our correspondence and can't wait to hug you in person someday.

To Kristin Anders—my plot bunny inspirer, plot hole fixer, rush job editor, ledge talker downer, and ultimate soul sister—I love you like no other. Thank you for all the things, ever.

To Laura Wright, my friend and ultimate sprinting partner, who offered me tons of advice on how to do this self-publishing thing and helped me make the whole package exactly what I want.

To Kerrie Legend for re-creating a cover that I absolutely love and for handling my craziness. I'm so thankful life brought us together!

To Erin Didion for not caring that I used her and her awesome pub in the book.

Don't miss out on Gina's other books:

FIGHTING FOR LOVE SERIES
SEDUCING CINDERELLA

Rules of Entanglement
Fighting for Irish
Sweet Victory
Stand-Alones
Tempting her Best Friend
Hot for the Fireman

PLAYBOYS IN LOVE SERIES

PLAYBOYS IN LOVE SERIES SHAMELESS

Ruthless
Merciless

Seducing Cinderella Excerpt

He walked his hand up the wall, drawing closer to her as he spoke. "Tell me what you want."

"I don't understand."

"There's a reason we're doing this. You want something. Don't think about the answer. I want you to *feel* the answer. Now," he said once he'd gone as far as he could and began to lean toward her, "tell me, what you want."

She licked her lips. Swallowed hard as his mouth got closer, but stayed just out of reach. "Right now?"

"Right this very instant."

"I want to kiss you so badly it scares me."

Her answer shocked the hell out of him—he'd been expecting her to say something along the lines of wanting her doctor—but he was too selfish to give a damn. "Then do something about it," he commanded.

Lucie grabbed the sides of his face and meshed her mouth on his. This time, saltiness left behind from her workout mixed with the strawberry taste of her lips. The combination was intoxicating, but it was nothing compared to the one-two punch he got when she swept her tongue over his upper lip.

Reid took that as an open invitation. Plunging his tongue inside her mouth was like tasting sweet ambrosia.

He hoped like hell his boxer briefs would do a better job of containing his growing erection than he did of containing the toe-curling groan that escaped his chest.

She pulled away, switching immediately into therapist mode. Although she wasn't usually so breathless when assessing him. He liked her affected like this. A lot. "This isn't a good idea, Reid. You need to stay focused with the stretches or you'll cause yourself more pain."

With his left hand on her chin, he dragged her attention away from his injury. "My shoulder isn't in pain right now, Lu. However, I can't say the same for another place of my anatomy."

He waited patiently for her innocent mind to catch up with his fiendish one wallowing in the gutter. To no avail. "I don't understand, where are you in pain?"

He hitched his left brow and quirked up a corner of his mouth in the universal smirk that said, "I'm thinkin' dirty." Now she'd get it in three...two...one...

A slight widening of those light gray eyes and a sudden interest in the ceiling above his head told him he was right on the money. He would've laughed at how charming he found the blush in her cheeks, but he wasn't exactly in the laughing mood. Nope. His mind had already hopped onto the one track that was headed straight for trouble. The fun kind.

"I know I'm not your type, Reid. You don't have to make things up to make me feel better about myself. I'm a big girl."

Was she fucking serious? She didn't think he was turned on by her? Now *that* was enough to piss him right the hell off. Abandoning the stupid stretch, he grabbed her ass in both hands and pulled her into his body.

Hard.

This time she gasped and planted her hands on his pecs in a feeble attempt to keep some semblance of space in the equation. Lucky for him, that wasn't the half he was concerned with obliterating everything between them but their clothes. And even those weren't a safe bet at this point. To prove it, he ground his pelvis forward, letting the hard length of his cock rub against the nerve-sensitive juncture between her legs.

"Feel that, Lucie? That's not how I react to women I'm not into. Believe me, there are other ways of teaching you these things. Less intimate ways." Ways that he should damn well be using. But instead he trailed one of his hands up her side and swept his thumb over her nipple, eliciting a wanton moan from her kiss-swollen lips. Even through the material of her sports bra and tank top he could see her nipple pucker and harden from his touch. He hissed in appreciation. "I just can't seem to leave myself out of this."

"Why not?" she said with just a hint of trembling.

Why not? That was the million-dollar question, wasn't it? Why couldn't he step back from her? Why was it that every time he pictured her doing anything with another guy, much less that asshole of a doctor she was so hung up on, his gut clenched like he'd just been sucker punched by a heavyweight?

"I don't know," he answered honestly. "All I know is I'm tired of fighting myself when I'm near you like this. So maybe I shouldn't. Maybe starting right now we come up with a new plan."

He wasn't sure if she realized it or not, but Lucie's hands left his chest and slid up behind his neck, allowing her breasts to mold themselves against him. Damn, he loved the way her softness gave way to his harder body.

"What are you suggesting?"

He dipped his head until they were so close they were sharing breaths, their noses lightly brushing as they danced around their overwhelming desire to fuse their mouths. "Maybe the best way to teach you how to seduce, is to let you feel what it's like to be seduced. And then let you try it out on someone who's not your eventual target. So you get any nerves out of the way."

"Like a trial run."

"Right. In the end I go back to reclaim my title like I want, and you bag what's-his-nuts, just like you want. No strings, no hard feelings. But in the meantime, we blow off some steam and get whatever the hell this is out of our systems."

"I suppose that makes sense. It's definitely a plan with merits." Her long fingers at his nape slipped up into the hair at the base of his skull as she tipped her head back, exposing the smooth expanse of her neck for his nibbling pleasure. "Oh, God." The prayer was a breathy whisper, just barely loud enough for him to hear, and made him grin with base satisfaction as he moved up to the space just behind her ear. She tasted like salted caramel, a combination it seemed he couldn't get enough of.

"So what do you say, Luce?" He nipped at her earlobe and then soothed it with a gentle suction in his mouth.

"I say—" Her answer was cut off by a gasp as he pushed her back the few inches to press her up against the wall.

"You were saying?" Reid prompted her to start her sentence again, knowing damn well he wasn't going to let her finish. It was too much fun interrupting her.

"I was saying that—*uhn!*" That time he ground himself over where he knew that sensitive little bundle was swollen and aching for some contact. "Damn it, Reid, yes, okay? I say yes to the new plan!"

"About damn time you spit that out." And with that, he attacked.

Gina L. Maxwell is a full-time writer, wife, and mother living in the upper Midwest, despite her scathing hatred of snow and cold weather. An avid romance novel addict, she began writing as an alternate way of enjoying the romance stories she loves to read. Her debut novel, *Seducing Cinderella*, hit both the *USA Today* and *New York Times* bestseller lists in less than four weeks, and she's been living her newfound dream ever since.

When she's not reading or writing steamy romance novels, she spends her time losing at Scrabble (and every other game) to her high school sweetheart, doing her best to hang out with their teenagers before they fly the coop, and dreaming about her move to sunny Florida once they do.

To subscribe to Gina's newsletters, click here.

Find Gina on the web:

www.ginalmaxwell.com | Facebook Fan Page | Maxwell Mob | Twitter | Instagram | Pinterest | Goodreads

Made in the USA
Lexington, KY
14 August 2019